BT

Count the Dead

Dawson is thrown off a freight train, half-dead. Then, when he finally finds himself riding into a nearby town, he is on a stranger's horse with a dead man roped behind the cantle.

Against all odds he finds himself a riding job with decent sidekicks. It looked good but trouble awaited him. Instead of tallying round-up steers he was forced to fight for his very life.

By the same author

Six for Laramie
Renegade's Legacy
Valley of the Guns

GUNFIGHT AT RAZOR EDGE

William R. Cox

GUNSMOKE

First published in the US by Paperback Library

This hardback edition 2013
by AudioGO Ltd
by arrangement with
Golden West Literary Agency

Copyright © 1970 by William R. Cox.
All rights reserved.

ISBN 978 1 471 32113 9

British Library Cataloguing in Publication Data available.

MORAY COUNCIL LIBRARIES & INFO.SERVICES	
20 35 56 84	
Askews & Holts	
WF WF	

Printed and bound in Great Britain by
MPG Books Group Limited

CHAPTER ONE

Sam Houston Booker pushed the small herd through the pass with an eye on thé black clouds hovering around Mount Cooper. He had only Pedro and the breed Santo to help him and the going was rugged and he feared a flash flood. He rode hard and halloed loud and they reached a high place exhausted and with night falling.

They made camp. There was no chuck wagon, only the pack horses, and there was no attempt to make a fire. They munched on jerky and cold biscuits. It was another low point—it had been all wrong from the start. Santo, who understood, huddled beneath his slicker and sat close to Sam while Pedro rode the early night watch over the sullen, dispirited bunch of skinny critters valuable only because among them was Clancy the surly but dependable seed bull.

"Damp, ain't it?" Water ran from Booker's hat brim and dripped monotonously between his worn boots.

"Si, señor." Santo was Mexican-Indian, a little jockey of a man. "Not good. We got trouble, I think."

"You sure about that sign?"

"Si, señor. Five, six vaqueros. Mexicano for sure."

Booker hated to believe it but Santo was a tracker who could read sign like a book. It was not only the wetbacks he had chivvied across the Rio and through Texas and into this Territory of New Mexico, it was the fact that all along the border there had been raids and counter-raids amounting almost to war. Truthfully, there was not anything he possessed which was worth the taking except Clancy the bull.

"Damn," he said. "Maybe the good Lord don't want a cowhand to get along in the world. Maybe what they say is right, thirty a month and found—busted up at forty. Maybe that's the way it's supposed to go."

"I think you try very hard. I think mebbe you might do."

"That's what you think?" His laugh was not pleasant. "Think about it. First we lose half the herd in the lightning and thunderstorm. Then I try to win some money for a stake in El Paso and they bust me out in a short card rangdoodle. So I shoot me a tinhorn and they chase me out of Texas."

"They no put you in hoosegow, though."

"Thanks to Jim Gillet. He was there and he's the Marshal and he's honest. But he had to tie a can to me."

"New Mexico is good. Grama grass. Not bad."

"I hope you're right. It wasn't my notion to go there."

Santo said softly, "Señor, the tinhorn. He was not the first you have gun down, no?"

Booker ran his hands along the hatbrim. "Be that as it may. He made his move."

It was not his first man, he had been unlucky that way. Somehow or other he had found himself pushed into corners whenever he tried to pull himself up by his bootstraps. He had gone up the trail as an orphan at fourteen and he had never enjoyed being bossed around by the herders so that right from the start he had wanted a spread of his own. Every time he made a beginning there had been men standing in his path. A few of them had been stubborn and Booker found out early that he had quick hands to match his temperament. Men had died and he had moved on, no richer, sometimes hunted. Now, at thirty, he owned a few head of puny cattle and one fine bull. He was going into unknown territory—and the poker game in El Paso had cleaned him out of cash.

Santo said, "We make it to high plain, we fine."

Booker regarded the breed in the gloom of the wet night. "You're a good hombre, you know that? You don't quit. Maybe you got luck, too. Maybe we will make it, at that."

"You make."

"If I do, you got a job for life."

"Me? Not so, I think."

"Why not?"

"Dunno," said Santo. "Long time since, you save me from gunny, no? No forget. Now you want ranchero. Cows, horses, mebbe lady? Not for halfbreed. I dunno why."

"The hell you say." But there was truth in it, the world could be a lousy place, he had his own prejudices like everyone else.

Working for wages was always the hard way to go. He had managed to save a few dollars and he had been lucky at poker one time which was when he had wisely bought Clancy the bull. Riding for the Bar Z in East Texas he had charged stud fees and Clancy had come through nobly, allowing the purchase of a few head of ordinary cattle. Next he had taken up the quest for land.

Then had come the troubles and the shootings and one thing and another. His father had also been redheaded and had been killed in a saloon fight. His mother had married again and departed for Florida and, it was to be hoped, a better life. His ancestry was of the hills of Tennessee, hence his middle name of Houston. He was rawboned and ruddy and he had never known a day of illness but he felt that his luck was uneven, not to be depended upon.

He said, "Five of 'em, huh, Santo?"

"For sure."

"They shoot crazy. They could kill Clancy."

"Si, they shoot crazy."

"I better ride with Pedro. No use tryin' to move tonight, the rain and all. Road might be closed ahead with a flood. Couldn't sleep anyhow."

"I sleep. Then I ride."

"Okay, Santo."

"Vaya con Dios," said the breed. "Go with God."

Booker saw to the picket line, made certain the little string was secure, saddled a grullo, the best of the lot, mounted and settled his poncho into place and rode into the driving torrent. Something Santo had said stuck in his mind, "mebbe lady?" He had known very few ladies and those from afar. He had known dance hall girls and plain whores but he would not know how to treat a lady. His had not been that kind of life.

But if a man could get land somehow or other and own a house and run cattle he would certainly want a woman. It was something to think about in the loneliness of the night watch. Would any kind of a lady take a second look at a red-haired, lanky cowman with no more than a McGuffy's Reader education and damn little table manners and no sweet talk easy to his tongue? It was improbable, yet he could not get it off his mind all through the wet night.

A mud wagon rested atop a small mesa, the patient team unhitched and blanketed against the storm. The rain did not inconvenience Piney Talcott in the least because he was inside the weatherproof light Concord coach, stretched out in the barber chair he had caused to be securely fastened to the floor boards.

Purchase of the "poor man's coach" had been a stroke of good luck. A man in Dodge City had been kindly and honest, warning of the rigors of the journey to New Mexico, advising him on all his outfitting. The sleek Remington rifle at his side, the comfortable Levis, walking boots, sombrero, wool shirt, all the appurtenances had proven the proper equipment for the final stages of the journey to the southwest. It was in Dodge City that he had learned the use of the long gun and had found to his great satisfaction that he was naturally a good shot. It was a long way back to New York City and the barbershop at midtown which had finally provided the comfortable stake that he had deemed necessary.

Of course he had used a rifle before, a dinky one in the shooting galleries of the city. Ever since he was a boy and had read the first stories in the Police Gazette in his father's shop, before his father had died, he had wanted to go west. It had been a good, clean shop and when the time came to sell to the Italian immigrant the price had been somewhat astonishing.

Then he had gone only so far as Chicago, which was booming and there he had barbered some more until he had increased his poke. After the Gem Of The Prairie he had gone downriver to St. Louis where he had played piano on the side and again added to his small fortune. Now he was all the way down here on his way to Silver City and the things he had heard about the Territory were encouraging.

In the beginning he had dreamed of being a cowboy. While gathering the customers, he had time to debate this. He was a small man and slight and he knew he would look taller on a horse. But he read in Leslie's *Illustrated Weekly* about the small pay and hard life of the cowhand and doubt assailed him.

It was when he had graduated to the financial pages and learned about ranching and the profits to be made shipping cattle and finally the refrigerated cars which allowed slaughtered beef to actually be transported eastward on the rails that he was galvanized into action and now his dream was to own a ranch, own horses, employ brownskinned, hardworking vaqueros. He would be good to them and pay the best wages to make sure they were the best he could employ. He would live like a king and try and make everyone around him live well.

He was in his thirties now and he had made it, he had

come finally to his west and he had found it beautiful. The great open spaces, the fine, exhilarating air, the beauty of the terrain was deeply and finally satisfying. He had brought his barber chair and the tools of his trade and cash that was sewed into the seat of the chair and he was vastly content and woke up eager for each new day.

He had not been hasty along the way. There was a deep streak of patience and caution within him. He had taken the time and trouble to learn all he could as he journeyed. He had learned the care of horses and weapons. He had studied the price of everything from land to cattle to harness to wages. Men talked in barber shops and polite questions drew lengthy answers. He had acquired cash and information with equal assiduity.

He had been frightened at times especially when the man had been shot and killed in the shop at Dodge City. And he had narrowly escaped an Indian raid on the road and had seen the tragic result of an attack upon an outlying ranch. He had ministered to the sole survivor, a small girl hidden in a root cellar, had conveyed her to town with news of the disaster.

He had thus far escaped combat on his own account. He had learned that a man must stand up for himself in this country, that he must never turn his back upon a fight, but he wondered uneasily at night how he would conduct himself if the occasion arose. He hoped he would have the courage of the heroes of paperback books he had perused with such thrills in his boyhood—but he was not at all certain that he could manage it.

He knew a lot about the western country and why men had come to it. He knew there were desperate refugees from the law. "GTT" they said, Gone To Texas and he had decided against the Lone Star State, choosing a promised higher freedom in New Mexico with its large Latin population. He knew about range wars over water or nesters. Perhaps that was a deep, inner reason why he had the deep desire to be of the west. He had never been, for some mysterious reason, like other people he had known. He had always felt somewhat apart from his kind.

His father had been a gentle, kindly man but the barber shop was his life. Mama Talcott had died when Piney was born, there were no other children. Life had been simple and even in tenor but one day followed the other with deadly dullness. Only magazines and books had provided release from the grind. He had spent the best part of his youth in among the printed pages.

Because of the barbering he had no young playmates. His father's pleasure had been to spend Sunday in Central Park feeding the swans and walking along the paths. Sometimes they would take the ferry to New Jersey for a day but this was a long and worrisome trip not to be undertaken lightly, replete with small fears and box lunches and concern about missing the last ferry and being late for opening of the shop on Monday morning.

It had not been enough. It was too small, a world too tight. From somewhere in his ancestry there was the sound of drums, of marching music, wild and free and Piney had listened. He could not have done otherwise.

The rain seemed to increase in fury on the mud wagon. He wrapped a slicker around him and went out the side door and looked to the horses. They were huddled together, heads down, rumps to the wind. There was little or no protection on the mesa but Piney had been warned. The road down below was swamped with flood waters. He stood a minute in the elements of the western country, alone but not lonely, filled with a deep satisfaction. He had come this far in safety, he would go on until he found a place, some place where he could purchase land, where he could acquire cattle. He had come to the threshold of his dream world.

There was a small private bar in the rear of the hotel in El Paso. John Stang sat across from Lige Tinsley and spun a four ounce shot-glass in his huge fist, making circles on the table top. He was Big John, his face, hard as rock, was wide and sunscorched, with knobs upon its planes, a face which had looked upon many things near and far. He was dressed for town—a string tie at the collar of his white shirt, a tailored jacket with stovepipe trousers, and embroidered walking boots.

Tinsley, more elaborately attired, was half his age, curly-haired, darkly tanned, handsome despite narrow-set eyes, flashing white teeth showing contentment as he smiled. He waited, lounging, pouring from a bottle.

Stang said, "It figures. We got to spread out. Rails is here, there, everywhere now, a circumstance I wouldn't of believed. We got all the graze we can get in Texas. We got that Wyoming land. If the grama grass is like you say, New Mexico is the next."

"It's ready made. The town is like Sunday School. We can start buyin' and work it quiet and own it all inside a year, just so we play our cards right."

"I don't want no war."

"Like I just said."

"You said. But you got a way about you, Lige. I told you many's the time. Don't hold nothin' back from me."

"John, I ain't holdin' back a thing."

"You done it before, got me into a rangdoodle."

"That was in the past. I learned."

John Stang studied the young man. Ten years ago there had been an Indian raid and this boy had survived only because a bunch of Stang's men had arrived in time. At fifteen Lige Tinsley had been fighting with the courage and skill of two grown men. Stang had taken him home and raised him. Childless, widowered, he had made the boy his own, in his own image. But there had been a quality deep inside, something in the Tinsley bloodstream which he had not been able to touch.

It was not temperament, Tinsley could get along with most people, he was quick to learn, he had brains enough to adapt. It was temper, a different matter. The dark spot lay there and when it came to life it burned with a flaring fire and then ensured trouble. It was part the temper and part a trickiness, a cuteness which Stang could not understand.

Since the War there had been wild times enough. Stang had swung a wide loop; he had taken and held land and cattle until he was one of the biggest in the country. He had ruled with an iron hand, hanged his rustlers, gunned down Indians, outlaws and anyone else who stood in his way including some honest men with more courage than brains. He was far from finished with wild times as he well knew but now he was in a different position, he was in the open, known, respected—and feared. If a man was feared he did not need to act. He needed only to ask, then demand, then threaten.

The trouble was that Lige threatened first and then wanted to act.

Stang said, "I keep tellin' you, we are now boss men. We talk low and slow and carry a big club. We don't have to swing that club. Lord knows we got enough to quit now. Seems like once you get started you can't stop reachin' for more in this here world. No question, we need new graze for the big herd. No question you're right about New Mexico. Only thing is—we got to stay out of a war if we possibly can."

"Look, John, there's this little bitty town, Quesada. Near enough to Silver City, far enough away. A few farms. A few little spreads. Man name of Mason, he's got a land development company and some property in town, he ain't rich, he ain't starvin', we can do business through him, he'll never know. If we rode in now and began tryin' like in Wyoming, then there could be trouble. Take our time, everything'll be peaches and cream."

"What about the law?"

"One man, name of Maylan, oldtimer."

"Maylan? Zeke Maylan?"

"That's right."

"He's honest as the day is long. Knew him 'way back at Ellsworth. Stubborn honest, he is."

"Sure. What of it? We buy our way in."

"How about water?"

Now Tinsley's eyes flickered, hooded. "Plenty of water."

"All right. Tell me about it."

"Well, they got this stream from the hills. There's wild mountains on the high plain, you know. Plenty of water."

"And who owns it?"

"They got an agreement. They share. We buy in, we got our share of the agreement."

"I see. You check this out with our lawyers in town?"

"I checked. They don't know New Mexico law but they're gonna look it up."

"But you seen the one point, didn't you?"

"I ain't dumb, John."

"If we don't buy out everything, we might have trouble with the water."

"No trouble. We could build a dam."

"We're takin' in a big herd. We need every drop of water we can get. You wasn't goin' to tell me about the water."

"John, it'll be all right. This town is a little piece of cornpone. This is there for the takin'. We don't need no gunnies, nothin'."

"We'll need guns."

"How do you know?"

"Because I know this country and you oughta know it

too, and I believe you do. There's always one sucker that'll hold out. There's always one cuss that won't sell."

"I checked 'em all. Nobody in that valley is that rich or that independent. You can buy 'em all."

"I'll talk to the lawyers."

"It's a good place, a good proposition, John."

"I'll talk to them."

Lige Tinsley showed his teeth again. "You sure do things careful these days. It's a fine way to be. I tell you I'm learnin'. I know you're right, every time you're right."

"The water. It's important." But he was mollified. He was close only to Lige, he wanted to be proud of the young man he had raised. He was tough enough to secretly admire a fighter, a good dirty fighter. He had become politic because that was the trend of the times, that was the way a man acted after he had striven to the top. He was cautious but there was still a lot of mountain lion in him. It was a question of knowing when and where to pounce.

"It'll be all right about the water. You'll see."

"No hurry. We got a year before the herd is so big we got to move it. In that time we can learn. You did a good job up there long as nobody recognized you for who you are."

"No chance of that. I was right careful."

The conversation was finished. Each man finished the drink before him, the barman came and put the bottle away, pocketing a coin. They arose and walked out of the hotel and toward Neal Nuland's bar and gambling palace. There had been trouble in El Paso; Marshal Stoudemire was dead of gunshot, Doc Cummings and his crowd were walking high, therefore they wore their Colt sixguns beneath their modish jackets. They walked tall, straddling in the fashion of horsemen, mincing, toes turning in.

A man came out of the Acme Saloon, weaving a bit, a tall, thin man with cavernous eyes. Lige Tinsley drew in his breath and slowed to a prowling pace. John Stang moved away into the shadows of an alleyway, cursing beneath his breath, whispering, "Steady, Lige, don't start nothin'."

"I'm steady." His hand was clawed slightly away from the butt of the gun beneath his jacket, he twisted to get position to draw as his left hand unbuttoned the coat.

The lean man squinted as the lights from the saloon fell across Lige Tinsley. He stood with feet apart, calling out.

"Tinsley?"

"I see you, Connor."

"You got your warning."

"I got your message."

Several pedestrians paused, listened, ducked for cover. A rider came down the street and tied to a rail, looked around, then slid behind his cayuse.

The voice of the man named Connor keened on the night air. "My wife, you dirty bastard, my wife."

"I wouldn't mention a lady's name, Connor."

"Her name? She's got no name now. Do you hear that?" The shakiness of alcohol was in the man's voice and demeanor.

John Stang called strongly, "You're drunk, Connor. You better go home and sleep it off."

"Drunk, am I?" The man screamed his rage and defiance. "I'm sober enough to see the two of you. Skunks smell better. You dirty, filthy, rotten hogs think you rule the country, don't you? Got everybody scared. I'll show you. . . ."

Connor suddenly dropped full length to the walk. He had a gun in his hand. He fired twice.

One bullet whistled close to John Stang, who made no move, knowing there were witnesses, knowing what would take place. He leaned against a wall, suddenly weary, watching Lige produce the sixshooter with deft, sure hands, hearing the sound of one shot, then nothing except the cries of people, the sound of footsteps hurrying to be at the death.

Jim Gillet came on the run, ex-Ranger, tough Marshal of El Paso, shotgun in hand. Stang stepped out into the light and spoke to him.

"Hello, Jim."

"John? What is this?"

"Connor fired twice. Lige fired once."

"Yes. I see."

"Plenty of people to testify."

"Connor wasn't smart." The ex-Ranger was stony-faced.

"No. He tried that old gunner's trick. He forgot to roll when he lit."

"Connor wasn't any gun."

"He was a drunk damfool."

"His wife was a nice enough gal, though."

"None of my business about his wife. Yours neither."

"That's right, John. None of our business. But I wouldn't want to be Lige Tinsley. Not for any money."

"Well, you ain't. You're a law officer. You do your job, I do mine."

"That's right, John. I'll take Lige in until the inquest."

"I'll see the judge and bail him out."

"Yes. That's the way it is."

"I'm sorry you don't like it, Jim. You're a helluva good man."

Lige came to where they stood, extending his revolver butt first. "Jim . . . He had two shots."

"Is he dead?"

"He's dead," Lige smiled. "He was shootin', y' see. Had to make sure."

"Is that Doc Brown with him?"

"That's the Doc. You want to walk me to jail before the crowd gets any bigger?"

"I'll take a look at him first."

Lige shrugged and looked at John Stang as the Marshal walked toward the dead man. "What could I do?"

"You coulda stayed away from Mazie Connor."

"Hell, I knew her before he married her. She worked the Acme, you know that."

"She was married."

"She was broke. Connor drank up his pay."

"No excuse," said John Stang. Yet he had not been without sinning as recently as his last trip east when the wife of that fat banker had become fascinated with the big man from the Wild West. He sighed. He would have to see the judge right away so that Lige didn't spend the night in the smelly El Paso hoosegow. . . .

The storm ceased before sunup and the ever-thirsty earth swallowed the flood and the sun struggled to mount the thrusting mountains. Sam Booker and the two herders managed coffee which they needed, and beans in a pan with lumps of thick bacon and some sweet slick on sourdoughs baked in the Dutch oven, a veritable feast. Clancy bellowed among the cows and the herd seemed rested despite the wet of the previous night.

Booker said, "Through that pass down yonder and up over the hill, there should be good grazin'. I hear tell the grama grass comes high to the bellies of the critters."

"It is true," said Santo.

Pedro was silent, a hard-bitten Mexican rider with no illusions and little gumption. He had been a peon in his own country and could not understand that his present position was any better or more desirable. He was a fair hand at packing and good enough with the cattle.

They got the herd moving, Pedro riding drag. The trail was clear all the way to the pass, which was a deep cut with high land ahead on either side and a small mesa on the east. To the west were rolling hills decked with pinon and yucca and buffalo grass. Clancy was fractious but Santo belted him with a rope's end and he rumbled along in the pack.

Atop the mesa was movement and Booker turned his full attention there, loosening his rifle in the scabbard. He was therefore ill prepared when Santo came riding and pointing and hallooing.

Five men wearing tasselled sombreros and short jackets came riding like fiends from the deep hole, shooting as they came from the hill to the west. They were slightly to the rear. Before Pedro could make a move they had riddled him with bullets.

The sound of the firing stampeded the herd. It thundered up the pass, away from the sound. Booker shot the two steers nearest him and yelled to Santo, who dismounted while his pony ran on free and up alongside. The carcasses of the dead steers shuddered as bullets struck them. The bandits rode past to form a circle and come in at full strength for one overwhelming charge.

Santo said, "Five. You count 'em? Like I say, five."

"Oh, sure," said Booker. "You were right. Hooray for you. Go to the head of the class."

"I go." Santo aimed with great care as the riders started their rùn. He squeezed off and one of the vaqueros screamed and tumbled to earth and lay still. The others scattered, Indian fashion.

"Four, now, is it not?" Santo was pleased.

"Nice shot, amigo."

Santo did not answer. Booker turned to look at him. Santo was on his side. Blood was streaming from his chest. He had been hit on the first attack but had managed to stay alive, stoic until he got his man. There was too much blood and Santo's breath came in gasps.

"Sonofabitch," said Booker. There were four of them and one of him. He reloaded his rifle and saw to the sixgun. If they had any sense they would take the cattle and run back for the border, leaving him afoot to his own devices. But they had lost a man and they were hotblooded and not too smart, he thought. Perhaps they had suffered in raids by Yanqui outlaws across the Rio and were out for vengeance. Perhaps some of the cattle in his own herd belonged to one of them. At any rate they were debating the best way to get to him and they were out of rifle range.

He would pick off as many as he could, he decided, then use the sixgun. Maybe he could get them before they killed him but he could not hope to remain whole in body while so doing, it wasn't in the cards. No, it was a question of time before they got somewhat smart and stalked him or starved him out or just plain picked him off from the rear. He could have told them a half dozen ways of doing it.

So it had come down to this after all the years of struggling against the world, he pondered, a lousy ambush in a canyon. Maybe right from the beginning it had been so decided—no way at all for the lone cowboy. It seemed ridiculous to come to this sort of an end. The brownskinned vaqueros were no real enemy, not badmen, not even lawmen thirsting for blood. They had their reasons for what they were doing and maybe the reasons were as good as those of Sam Houston Booker.

At least he had made a sashay at being somebody, he thought, watching them spread out and again begin their Indianlike tactic of riding around him. He estimated the range and looped a shot at them and a horse went down. The rider scrambled free. He was out of range and Booker wasted a bullet, reloaded his rifle. The sun came through over the serrated peaks of the mountains, and a light haze and reflections from the quartz in the rock bestowed an eerie purple haze on the scene in the canyon.

It would be hot in an hour and he resented lying there behind the stinking carcasses of the steers. Santo breathed one last time beside him and was still and that saddened him. He had thought to hold onto the little man in the time ahead, the time he had thought to buy through one means or another. Now it looked as though there wouldn't even be anyone around to bury either one of them.

Now two of the Mexicans were angling up the side of the little mesa, attempting to get high gun on him. The man afoot and the other one went to the rear to encircle him and get a crossfire going. They kept out of range. They had finally realized the situation and now he was in real trouble. If he had known a prayer he would have uttered it.

He swung his rifle one way and the other, seeking a sure target. The two on the mesa were creeping closer but not close enough. The two in the rear were mounted and waiting for the moment to make their charge. They were very brave men. They were willing to risk their lives for the cattle, but mainly for Clancy, he knew. A good seed bull would make them rich in Mexico, as rich as vaqueros could ever become.

The horsemen received a signal from the mesa. They uttered shrill yells and spurred their horses. At the same moment the men on the hillside began to move down, their rifle barrels glinting in the weird light. It was impossible to cover all of them. He fired uphill, then turned to scatter the ozone with shots close to the oncoming horsemen. It was now a matter of moments.

He swung back and saw what had to be a mirage in the purple daylight. There was a man atop the mesa. He held a long gun in his hands. He was hesitating, uncertain but he kept coming, peering down at the combatants. He wore a conventional flat sombrero and Levis and was positively not a Mexicano. Booker almost screamed to him that he should take the two afoot within his range, at the same time wheeling to meet the charge of the vaqueros on their horses. He shot one of them in the chest and saw him go backwards, saw the other veer off.

He turned back. The man in Levis was kneeling, taking plenty of time. There was a faint bow wave of sound. One of the stalking vaqueros threw out his arms and tumbled head over heels down the hillside. The other panicked, stood up, thrusting his gun toward the newcomer, firing wildly.

Booker again turned to his rear. The mounted man was shooting as he came. Booker fired twice. The second shot brought down the horse. He caught the rider as he tried to run, hitting him between the shoulder blades.

When he again looked eastward into the odd light the man atop the mesa was firing rapidly, pumping the Remington. The last remaining Vaquero stumbled in flight and fell forward. The rescuer stood, irresolute, then slowly began sliding down the hill, his boots slithering on loose shale. He paused at the first body, removed his hat, wiped his brow with his sleeve. At the second body he took one look, then turned away.

Booker arose, flexed his knees and began walking toward his rescuer. The light enveloped them both. Relief flooded Booker, he shouted loud and strong.

"You must've been sent by heaven—or the devil."

"I—well—it happened so quick. I guess I'm scared, now."

"Nothin' to be scared of, they're all down."

They walked slowly toward each other. Sam stuck out his hand, "Sam Booker."

"Piney Talcott."

"Well, howdy and thanks a plenty." The light changed as the sun mounted and he stared beneath the brim of the man's flat hat. He gulped. He said, "I be damn. You . . . you're a . . . you're a . . . nigra!"

CHAPTER TWO

All day long they labored at disagreeable, arduous tasks. After the first shock of recognition Sam Booker tried very hard to treat Piney Talcott as another human being, one to whom he owed his life and on the whole he thought he succeeded. He was of Tennessee and Texas but he had always been different, a man apart. The shootings had made him somewhat of an outcast, which made it easier to swallow prejudice inborn through generations.

Besides which, he thought as they buried the dead and searched the bodies and rounded up the remaining horses and did all that was required, this man was also different from the niggers he had encountered. There was no "Yassuh, Boss" dialogue, there was no deference in attitude. The slight man had huge forearms and biceps and was stronger than he appeared and he moved with economy and deftness despite the unfamiliarity of the work.

He said a little prayer over the trench in which they finally placed the corpses. His dignity impressed Booker, who knew no prayers. He rode well enough to help round up the herd and he was not frightened by Clancy the bull and his antics. When some sort of order was restored he sat down a moment alongside Booker and removed his hat and rubbed his kinky hair.

"I never shot at a man before. I'm still somewhat scared and shaky."

"Scared sometimes fights better," said Booker. "Seems to me you're some kind of a man, Piney."

"I never harmed anyone in my life. Didn't think I could, truth to tell. I don't think I like it."

"You ain't from down South, I take it?"

"I was born in Virginia. My grandfather was a slave, the Talcott plantation. Papa was a house servant, a freeman and a barber. I was raised in New York City."

"Went to school, a man can tell. You—you're real different. Y'see all niggers—nigras—I ever knowed was field hands. Or maybe a cowboy or two, not much account. Buffalo soldiers, lots of sand but mostly drunk and sometimes bad. The South includin' Texas is bad for black folk."

"I heard. So I came to New Mexico."

"Barberin'?" It was easier all the time to talk to this unassuming, natural man who took it for granted they were equals.

"Maybe." Talcott shook his head. "I don't understand it, it seems terrible, but I'm awful hungry all of a sudden."

"All I got is some cold vittles."

"I can do better at the wagon."

"Oh. You got a wagon?"

"Up yonder. I'd be honored if you'd join me, Mr. Booker."

"No call for that, Piney. Not 'mister.'. . . Sam." As they began the ascent of the mesa he went on earnestly, "No, I mean that good. I mean I lost a man today, we just put him away. Name of Santo. Half Injun, some Mex, some Nigra."

"I noted that you sorrowed over the darkskinned man."

"He was a good one. Me, I'm southron. But they don't cotton to me much in Texas and some other places."

"I guess I understand."

But he was quiet and reserved, thoughtful. When they reached the mud wagon Booker stood with arms akimbo, then went close, examining everything, then looked over the horses.

"You got some outfit, Piney. I swan to ginney, you are really some kind of man."

"There are all kinds of black men." He produced canned fruit, they made a fire and cooked meat and ate pilot biscuits. They sat together on the wagon pole, each with his thoughts. Neither wanted to pursue the matter of race, of differences between them and of the outside world.

When they had finished and cleaned up Talcott asked, "How are you going to drive the herd alone?"

"I been thinkin' on that. Clancy the bull, he's about all I got except ten dollars and the few pesos we took off the vaqueros. The skinny old cattle, I could turn 'em loose and maybe come back for 'em after I sold Clancy."

"You want to sell the bull?"

"Piney, I'd rather sell my right arm. But I'm outa cash. I need land, a cabin. Had I enough to get a start, Clancy would get me some place given time."

"Did you hope to find land up ahead?"

"Town name of Quesada. There's a valley full of grama grass, so Santo said. Not too many people. Thought I might trade for some graze—somethin'. A long shot, but a man has to try. I been all my life tryin' to get cattle and land together."

"You say it can be done in Quesada Valley? If you had land, that is?"

"Could be. If a man had cash he might buy in. Rest of it is know how and a bull like Clancy."

Talcott stood straight, his brown eyes fixed on Booker. "Let me get this straight. If you don't have cash you must sell your bull. Without him, you got nothing but the herd. The herd isn't valuable without the bull. Is that right?"

"That's all of it in a nutshell."

"Mr. Booker. . . ."

"Sam, damn it, Sam. You saved my life and you're a man I like. More I see of you the more I like your style."

There was another silence. Then Talcott smiled widely. "Why, that's a fine thing to say. You like me. That's fine."

"It's true, damn it."

"Well . . . Sam. I have cash. Quite a lot of cash."

"You what?"

"There's money in barbering. I saved mine."

"So you got cash?"

"I have."

"In the wagon?"

"In the wagon."

"Then you ain't got much sense. Supposin' I put a gun on you right now?"

"Then my troubles would be over—and yours just beginning."

Booker thought that over for a minute. "See what you mean."

"On the other hand, you need help. Supposing we put my wagon and me on the drag? Think it would help?"

"You know what the drag is?"

"I've learned something along the way."

"If you could jump down and ride if it was necessary, it might could work as far as Quesada."

"Good. Now I have to tell you. I had a dream."

"A dream?"

"You and me, we both had the same dream. Land, cattle, a place to build."

"That's what I always wanted."

"I've got cash. You've got a herd."

"You mean that for sure, what you're sayin'?"

"I'm a black man. Think on that."

"Why should I? A man comes down off a mesa when I'm about wiped out. He offers to buy land for my cattle, land I got no way of gettin' for myself. I'd be worse'n a dumb fool to look at his color."

"You have to be mighty sure."

"New Mexico ain't Texas for one. And for two I've taken a likin' to you before you mentioned about money. Right?"

"If you believe it."

"My cattle against your money? It's a deal."

"Your cattle and your white skin plus my cash. And I'm not planning on being a silent partner."

"Why should you?"

"Many a black man has hidden behind a white partner in this country."

Booker said honestly, "Look, I know a lot of people might look cockeyed. Yeah. But they'd mostly be nothin' people. Now I got to tell you somethin' else. I got run outa Texas for shootin' a crooked gambler. So where do I stand?"

"Higher than any black man."

"Folks may think so. I think the other way. Take another look. I'm down there gettin' ready to depart this here earth. You come along and now you're offerin' to buy land for my cattle. Fifty-fifty. Right?"

"There can be no other partnership but even-Steven."

"Right. My sentiments exactly. So you come along in the nick of time. Now, how do you figure such a circumstance?"

"No use to figure, is there?"

"Right. It's a circumstance." He extended a heavy but supple hand. "Shake?"

Black hand met freckled hand. It was all the contract they ever had between them.

They drove the herd to the very edge of town. Quesada was larger than they had thought and from a distance looked new and shining under the morning sun. Sam Booker saddled the grullo and prepared to ride in.

"You get along with Clancy," he said. "Just ride easy around 'em and if you know a tune, hum it. Critters is peculiar that way, they take to singin' and the like."

"They'll be fine," said Piney Talcott. He had a *reata* on his saddle; he sat very straight and tall and proud.

"I'll find us a boy or two to watch 'em when I get the lay of the land."

"Just take your time." He was happier than he had been since the days of dreaming in the barber shop in New York. He was actually a cowboy for a day. He watched his partner take the road to town and rode the pony from the remuda around the perimeter of the herd. Clancy gave him a low rumble which was friendly and he reined in to scratch between the ears of the bull. The promised land lay ahead and the day was full of unadulterated pleasure.

In two hours his thighs ached from the unaccustomed exercise. He dismounted at the mud wagon and tied up. The road was deserted, no one was in sight. He opened the side door, recollected himself, took his Remington from the boot and leaned it beside him. Then he climbed in beside the barber chair and took sharp, pointed shears from a kit. He snipped away at threads on the seat of the chair, occasionally checking on the surroundings.

He found the money belt and pulled out his shirt and adjusted it around his waist. There was seven thousand dollars in the belt. He found needle and thread and sewed the plush of the seat back in place with quick, neat stitches. He heard the sound of a horse approaching and slid down, grabbing for the rifle.

Sam Booker rode in. Following him was a young man on a shaggy, tough looking pony. Piney went to meet them.

They swung down and Sam said, "This here is Ricco Camponetta. Meet my pardner, Piney Talcott."

The youth was swarthy and handsome and about him was a look of open spaces, a free look. "Howdy, glad to meetcha."

"His papa's the smithy," said Sam. "Ricco, he's a huntin' man and somewhat of a cowhand, he allows."

"Anything but that stinkin' forge," said Ricco cheerfully. "You go right on in and see Mr. Mason. I can handle it here for you."

Sam said, "Reckon we'd take the mud wagon. That sound okay?"

"Why not?"

They hitched up Piney's team. Sam probably thought the cash was still in the wagon, Piney thought amusedly, he wanted to be sure they had the money on hand for a quick deal. Redhaired men were like that, he had learned, they were sudden, as the western expression had it.

Sam sat on the edge of the seat of the wagon and talked, excited. "Tom Mason's our man, all right. I rode past his place. Camponetta's a friendly hombre, he said there was a place for sale, didn't know the price. I rode out a ways. The grama grass is belly high west of town. Only thing is, this land has got to cost a heap."

"How much is a heap?'

"Thousands. There's a bank we could look into. If we got enough for a down payment."

"We have enough."

"If you say so." He was very dubious. "It's rich land in this here valley, fine and rich."

It was a one street town but there were many side streets also, a big General Store, a Wells Fargo office, a jail with the Marshals dwelling attached in the rear, a carpenter shop, a small hotel, two saloons and a cantina for the Mexican people, a dress shop, a private bank, carpenter shop, the smithy, a generous scattered assortment of big and little adobe houses and a few of brick and frame. The Mason Land Development Company was next to the bank and across from the General Store. There was an empty store next to the General Store. Piney took it all in with an eye practised through the long ride across country.

A tall thin man came from the Development Company. A small thin boy ran past him and stared. The man looked the wagon over, opened his eyes at the sight of the barber chair.

"Don't tell me Quesada is to be honored with the services of a barber!" he said. "I am Tom Mason and I happen to have a shop for rent. Right across the street."

Sam climbed down and said, "More like we're looking for a spread for sale." He introduced himself and Piney. "My partner and I are lookin' to buy."

Mason shook hands, hesitated, looking again at Piney. "Partners . . . H'mmm, I see. Now, what kind of a ranch were you looking for?"

The boy came and stood looking. He was pale and wore steel rimmed spectacles. "That man's black, papa. The other's red. Red and black."

"Hush, Tommy." Mason spatted the boy's rear and sent him inside. "I'm afraid a lot of people might . . . well, out of the mouths of babes and sucklings. Still, it is none of my business. We do need a barber. . . . But about the ranch. I have a place out west a piece. Prime grama grass, some timber. How many head do you expect to run?"

"Right now a couple hundred. Later who knows?"

"This place is somewhat larger than you need right now. However, Mr. Parker at the bank might be interested in a mortgage."

Piney spoke. "No mortgages, please, sir."

"Ahh, then I would require a goodly amount of cash." Mason's voice held a touch of Yankee twang, softened by usage in the Southwest.

"How much cash?"

"Well, at least six thousand."

Sam said, "That's a heap of money."

"Would you take five?" Piney was asking.

Mason hesitated. "Maybe you'd like to see the place."

"I sure would," said Sam. "I'd like to see a hell of a lot of place away out here for that kinda money. I'd like to see a house on it and a well and a barn and a corral and a hell of a lot else."

"It's a nice little ranch. I'd be glad to show it to you."

Piney said, "I think we should look at it."

"Anything else hereabouts, maybe cheaper?" asked Sam.

"The valley's full up. Quiet people, farmers, just a few cattle ranches. No big outfits. There's a fence to keep the cattle from the farms. It's like I say, peaceful country."

"I'm plumb peaceable," Sam assured him. "Climb in. Show us this place which is worth all that money."

They drove to the west, past people who looked with mild curiosity then went their way, past the smithy where a squat, broad man waved to them. The road widened and now there was colla, ocatillo, late blooming barrel cactus and green, green grama all spreading to rolling hills beyond which towered mountain range after mountain range. This was the fertile high plain and beyond were the mines and Silver City and Santa Rita and the copper pit.

"We're passing the Badger ranch, called B-Dash-Z," Mason told them. "Next door is Courtney's Rocking-L. My place—it was owned by a man named Beasley, he couldn't make it, a shiftless fellow—is back off the road, sort of in-between, in a V, you might say. It's an odd formation of land, the hills come down into it. There's the feeder stream, you can see it coming down from Little Bear, clear mountain water."

"I see it," said Sam. "It runs sidewindin', don't it?"

"Across the ranches," said Mason. "There's an agreement makes it free for everyone."

"Unless somebody builds a dam."

"The agreement is registered. These people, Courtney, Badger, the others, they're more farmer than rancher, though they run prime cattle. No fighters here, Booker."

"That makes me real happy. Only thing bothers me around here is the prices."

Mason said, "If you'll turn right at the next bend we'll be on the road to the place we want to see."

They wound up a long lane toward the hills. They came to a gate and Mason opened it and got back into the wagon. The road was rutted and in poor condition. There was no sound, a strange stillness indicated that the ranch was deserted. But the grama grass was thick and green and the sun shone bright overall. Piney drew in his breath and let Sam drawl against the cost of everything. They came to the buildings, which were set against the hill, sheltered from the north winds. The house, set apart from barn and sheds and corral, was adobe, fair-sized. The hill was flat, like the mesa from which Piney had descended to meet Sam Booker. A ditch ran along its edge and there was a well and a little creek besides, burbling happily to the nearest field.

They got down and looked around. The house needed repair, windows were broken, a door sagged, but inside the structure was well arranged, with a pump in the kitchen, and a fireplace containing an iron stove. There were two bedrooms and a big, wide parlor.

The barn needed even more work, the roof was blown off in one corner. The other buildings seemed secure enough.

Mason said, "You can see it all from the top of the hill, there."

They climbed up the steep slope. The grass was a carpet running east and west and toward the main road. Sam could find no fault with it.

"Twenty dollars an acre is cheap," Mason told him. "This is not wild country. The buildings are worth half of it."

"The buildings need work. We need a year to build a beef herd. We got to pay wages. It'll take a lot more'n five thousand."

"Six thousand."

Piney was removing his belt. Mason's eyes bugged out as he saw the clean, crisp banknotes. Sam stepped back, unbelieving, closing his mouth tight against outcry.

Piney said, "Five thousand, Mr. Mason. Which leaves enough to fix up and maybe buy a few Herefords." He looked at Sam. "I have a notion. That shop across from Mr. Mason's office. Take a little to fix it, too. But I could barber four days a week. Make enough to pay wages, do you think, Mr. Mason?"

"The men go all the way to Silver City for fixing. Otherwise their wives have to put a bowl over their heads and snip away. I'd be pleased to have a barber in town. Ten dollars per month will pay for the shop."

Piney said, "Against the fixing?"

"You men drive a hard bargain."

"We're trying to start right," said Piney. "Without too much risk. It's better for the town that way, isn't it?"

Mason said, "Let's go back to the office and get a pencil and paper and figure."

Sam said, "A real sharp pencil."

By nightfall they were back at the camp to eastward of Quesada. Ricco was waiting. Piney gave him two dollars and Sam held his elbow a moment.

"We're goin' to work the Mason place—Beasley place, whatever you call it. You want a job?"

"Part time?"

"Full time."

"I work only part time. Accordin' to the huntin'," said Ricco. "I can get you a man full time."

"A good man?"

"Not many think so. But there ain't many to hire in the Valley. Delaney's old but he's handy and he's a cattleman."

"Bring him out tomorrow?"

"Right," said Ricco. He waved the two dollars. "Tonight I drink some vino, see my gal. Tomorrow I see you at the ranch."

They sat down and pored over the deed of ownership to the ranch. The legal language was muddy but they could understand that they owned the land.

Sam said, "You're some game galoot, Piney. Even that banker was some taken aback when you slapped down all the cash. More'n he seen at one time in a long while, I bet."

"It was spent for what it was intended." Piney was glowing with pleasure, touching the property deed, running his fingers over it. "Money is good when it can buy a dream."

"I thought up a name for us," said Sam.

"A name?"

"And a brand. We got to register a brand for the two of us."

"That's right. I hadn't thought of that."

"Razor Edge," said Sam.

"Razor Edge?"

Sam took a stick and drew a rough outline in the dirt. "See? I'll have Camponetta make us some irons. It's kind of fancy but I like it. Okay?"

"Razor Edge." He rolled the words in his mouth.

"You're the barber, see? And we made a sharp deal I do believe. You like it?"

"I like it. I like it very much," said Piney.

It wasn't easy at first. Some people like Mueller of the General Store, an emigrant Prussian, tried to be uppity with Piney and Sam had to get them told. He was neither polite nor ugly, he just told these folks. He told them Piney was not only his partner but his friend, that his life had been saved by the Negro and he meant to repay the debt one way or another before he died.

He had Mueller by the throat against the wall outside the store while he was orating in this fashion. A gaunt, stoop-shouldered man wearing a star on his loosely fitted vest came to listen and look on. With him was a leggy girl with amazing auburn hair who watched with amusement and approval.

When Sam had paused for breath in his loud oration the older man said mildly, "I take it you don't mean to harm Mr. Mueller, do you, Mr. Booker?"

Sam released the bulky grocer. "Oh, no, Marshal. I was just hintin' around."

"I believe you done made yourself clear."

Mueller said, "He should be arrested already. Look what he done to my shirt."

The Marshal said, "Mr. Booker got you told, Otto. You never been too polite anyhow. You're gettin' rich off the Valley, maybe you should learn some manners also. Insultin' a new citizen, that's no way to act."

Mueller resorted to gutturals, retreating inside the store to mumble at his small, thin wife, a lady much pitied in Quesada. The Marshal winked at Sam and turned to the girl.

"Alicia, this here is the new fella takin' over the old Beasley place. Sam Booker, my daughter Alicia Maylan."

Her eyes were wide and blue, her smile broad. She wore a man's shirt and a divided skirt and boots on feet that were generous enough to support her height, which was above that of the average woman. There was a direct quality in her, she frankly looked Sam over from head to shabby boots.

"How do you do, Mr. Booker? Welcome to Quesada."

"My pleasure, ma'am." He was always uncomfortable around ladies but this girl was something else again. She instilled confidence by her interest in him.

"Ricco has been telling me about you. We'd be pleased to have you and your partner for supper while you're getting settled."

"Why, thank you, ma'am. But we'll be awful busy for a spell."

"Any time you're ready," she said. She walked away toward the livery stable across the street.

Marshal Maylan said, "Goin' for her horse. That gal is a pure nature lover. She and that Ricco ride the hills like there's gold in 'em."

"I'm hopin' to keep Ricco busy for awhile. Can you tell me where I'll find a man named Jack Delaney?"

"Might try Finnegan's saloon. You thinkin' of hirin' old Jack?"

"You reckon it's a bad idea?"

"It's a good notion. Help is scarce in the Valley, people keep right busy. Thing is, old Jack's got a little stake. He won't stir unless he takes to a man."

"Choosey, eh?"

"You might say. One other thing—Joe Beasley's still around town. Mason had to foreclose on him, y' know. Beasley's no account but he's big and mean. If he had any brains he wouldn't have lost the ranch. He might take it poorly that you're movin' in."

"Now that's too bad," said Sam. "I wouldn't want any trouble, startin' out in a new town."

Maylan's manner altered slightly. "Tell you the truth, I wouldn't want to see gun play."

"Yeah." Sam sighed. "Reckon you know about me, eh?"

"Nothin' real bad. Us oldtimers, we get to know things. The west is calmin' down. Law officers exchange stories, know what I mean?"

"Jim Gillet?"

"Jim gives you a good name. But he says you're gunquick. That is, someone starts it, you like to finish things up."

"True," said Sam. "Things generally work that way."

"I don't like shootin'. Ain't had any in some time."

"Look, Marshal, I come here to settle down. Last thing in the world I want is a gunfight." He unbuckled his belt. "Maybe you better take care of this for me until I ride out."

The Marshal smiled, accepting the offer. "That's right decent of you. I wouldn't have asked. But—Beasley may be in Finnegan's saloon also. Beasley's no shakes with a gun. He's a fisticuffer."

"Might's well get it over with," said Sam. "I sure appreciate the warnin'."

"We'll get along. Lishia liked you, I could tell. Lishia don't make too many mistakes." The Marshal nodded pleasantly and strolled toward his office, jail and domicile.

Sam finished loading supplies into the mud wagon. The barber chair had been removed and placed in the shop. Piney and a Mexican boy and girl were cleaning and scrubbing. Sam stopped in the doorway to the establishment. The chair sat in splendor, there was a small mirror on the wall, and Casper the carpenter had installed shelves for barber tools and supplies.

"How you doin'?" he asked.

Piney said, "Amazingly well. I'll be open for business by the time we're set at the ranch. You ready to go now? Aurelio and Inez can handle things here."

They were brother and sister, in their late teens, handsome, olive-skinned, and well-spoken. They smiled shyly at Sam and continued their labors.

Sam said, "I got another errand. The wagon's loaded. You keep on here and I'll be back."

Finnegan's Saloon was at the end of the block. It was a low-ceilinged place dedicated to the workingman, the cowboy and farmhand as opposed to the bar in the hotel which was patronized by owners, foremen and visiting firemen. Finnegan was a wizened little man in his forties with one walleye, which he fixed upon Sam with some uneasiness.

At the far end of the bar a barrel-bodied man leaned, a beer in front of him. At a nearby table sat a medium-sized, bowlegged, grizzled individual whose seamy skin connoted years of outdoor exposure in all kinds of weather.

Sam said, "Jack Delaney?"

The man at the table said, "I'm him."

"Like to palaver with you." He turned to Finnegan. "Whatever the gent's drinkin' and a whiskey for me, please."

From the end of the bar the big man said in a whiskey voice with a nasty edge, "So you're the man who took my ranch."

"I don't think I know you," said Sam. "Buy you a beer?"

"Name of Beasley. Joe Beasley. And you can keep your beer. Damn Texans comin' in, takin' a man's property."

"Sure," said Sam. "Payin' cash for it, too."

"Bad enough a damn Texan but when he brings a stinkin' black son of a bitch nigger as his pardner, that's the end."

Sam said, "Hold the beer, Mr. Finnegan." He walked slowly down to the end of the bar. "My partner's name is Mr. Piney Talcott. He's a gentleman. I'd appreciate it if you keep that in mind."

The big man came away from the bar. He had short, powerful arms and huge fists. "No damn nigger is a gentleman nowhere, nohow. What do you think of that you sand-slappin' Texas basttid?"

"I don't think much of it." Sam hit him in the belly.

The big man roared and swung. Sam was no fist fighter but he knew enough to duck and plant another punch to the belly which looked as though it had retained much of the beer imbibed by Beasley.

The big man gasped but grabbed hold of Sam's right wrist and swung. Sam went across the room and over the table just as Delaney vacated his chair. Slamming against the wall he felt the breath go out of him. He scrambled and managed to get to his feet, slightly unsteady, as Beasley came again. He was unable to duck a blow which caught him alongside the head and sent him reeling to the rear of the bar.

Delaney was against the wall, watching, expressionless. Finnegan had a bung starter in his hand but seemed willing to let nature take its course so long as there was no damage to the stock.

His back to the wall, his brains addled, Sam saw the burly man charging at him. He instinctively raised his knee and thrust with the toe of his boot. He luckily caught a knee-cap. Beasley stopped as though shot, bellowing with pain, reeling backward. Sam made himself follow, right fist poised. The leg buckled and Beasley fell against the bar. Sam hit him a glancing punch on the jaw that spun him so that he faced Finnegan.

Still roaring, Beasley snatched the bung starter from the startled barman. Sam retreated two steps and stood his ground, breathing hard. Beasley swung the heavy, water-hardened club. Sam sidestepped. Limping, Beasley followed him.

Sam's foot slipped in the sawdust. Beasley rolled in, raising the bung starter high, aiming for the skull, a blow that would certainly have killed the victim. Sam tried to jump aside and slipped again. He was on one knee, he could see the club coming down, he threw up his arms in a vain attempt to protect himself.

Beasley suddenly pitched forward. Sam moved and let the big body hit the floor alongside him, managed to get to his feet, gasping. Jack Delaney was holstering an old-fashioned long-barreled Colt .45.

Finnegan said, "Good shot, Jack. Don't want no killin' in here. The Marshal wouldn't like it none."

From the doorway Marshal Maylan said, "For once you're right, Finnegan. Seems like there's been a bit of trouble."

Sam said, "Nothing to speak of, Marshal."

"You got quite a lump aside your head."

"Yeah." Sam gingerly touched it. "Ran into somethin' or other."

Maylan looked at Jack Delaney. "That the way you saw it?"

The old man's voice had a youthful timbre. "When I like a man's style I go along with what he says."

"Then I reckon poor Beasley's just drunk."

"Mean drunk," said Finnegan. "You might cool him off for awhile, Marshal."

"I might do that." Maylan sat down at the table, pulling it into place. "When he wakes up, that is. He's too big to haul around."

Sam said, "He's big, all right . . . Delaney, could I talk to you outside?"

"Don't mind us," said the Marshal. "See y'all later."

On the street Delaney examined the Concord. "I mind these from days when I was scoutin' for the army."

"Lately it seems I been spendin' a lot of time thankin' people for savin' my hide," Sam said. "I do appreciate."

"Give you a gun you'd be okay," said Delaney. "Beasley, he's a fist man. Not that you done bad 'til you slipped."

"I didn't do good," Sam said ruefully. "What I wanted in there, I wanted to ask if you'd work for us at Razor Edge."

"What I was gonna say was no thanks."

"Well, much obliged anyway," said Sam.

"But seein' your style, like I say, I changed my mind. I get forty and found, I'm a top hand."

"You got a horse?"

"I got me a cuttin' pony is the best there is. I got a rope and my own guns. I got a little money in the bank, I don't have to work. But a man needs somethin' to do," said Delaney. "If you hire other hands, I'm foreman, right?"

"Only Ricco, he's all we need and him part time."

"I know. Ricco told me."

"Sure." Everything got around fast in a town as small as Quesada, Sam knew. "Ricco's handy with tools. We need a cattleman right now most of all."

"You got one. See you at—what did you call it?"

"Razor Edge."

"For the barber." Delaney nodded. "He's a right nice man, your pardner. Had a talk with him this mornin'. Only thing worried me was you."

"You mind sayin' why?"

"I seen gunfighters. I seen 'em try and settle down. Seldom do they make it. If you'd a had a gun when you was down and Beasley was comin' with the bung starter there wouldn't be no Beasley. Nor no Razor Edge because Maylan woulda turned agin you quick. And Maylan is all the law the Valley's got."

"And Valley people are law-abidin'?"

"Good place for you and me to settle down," said Delaney. He tapped his gun butt. "This here old thing ain't even loaded. I carry it for an equalizer, like just now. See you at the ranch, then. Razor Edge."

Sam watched him walk toward the livery stable where Alicia Maylan had gone. Delaney hobbled a little as though he had ridden one too many broncs into submission, but there was a swagger to his shoulders.

It was time to get Piney and stock the larder, and help Ricco and get things in order. It was a beautiful day and the air of the high plain was brisk and clean. It was, as Delaney had said, a good place to settle down. If they had a good year, one good year. . . .

CHAPTER THREE

It was the anniversary of the arrival in Quesada of the cowboy and the barber. Piney Talcott stood in the doorway of his shop and admired the weather. It had been a fine year and the day had dawned as though all the years would be the same, prosperous and happy.

Out on Razor Edge the roundup would be in progress but Sam had to make it to town for a small celebration. Piney smiled and spoke with the citizenry passing by. He knew them all now, and they knew him. Young Tommy Mason was rolling a hoop up and down Main Street, not expertly but happily, kicking up small clouds of dust.

Marshal Maylan and his daughter paused, smiling.

"When's Sam coming in?" asked Maylan.

"When he can get loose, I guess. He hates to take time off these days."

"And I baked a cake!" expostulated Alicia.

"I think Piney's funnin' you," said her father. "I imagine Sam's rarin' to get here in time for the supper."

"He did insist I have the water hot and plenty of Pinaud's Eau de Cologne," said Piney.

"I wanted to have a dance at the town hall," Alicia said. "Sam thought it would be too much."

"Never do see you at the Saturday dances," the Marshal said to Piney.

"Never did learn." He easily evaded the unspoken question. People had been wonderful to him but he was determined to "keep his place" in certain areas. It wasn't only Otto Mueller who did not fully accept him. He knew why Sam had refused to hold a dance on their anniversary and Alicia knew it also.

She said, "Piney won't even play piano for us, only for you and me and Sam."

"I'm afraid few would appreciate my playing. I learned on the river, Kansas City, lowdown gospels. It's Negro music. You're the only ones who enjoy it."

"It's beautiful," she said. "I'm learning from you. I'll surprise you some day."

They went on to the General Store to make last minute purchases for the supper at their house that evening. The other invited guest, Tom Mason, came across the street, bent-shouldered, his face solemn, beckoning Piney inside the shop.

There was a pool table in a side room now, and a partition behind which was a public bath. It was all spic and span and bright. Piney waited for the land developer to sit in the chair but Mason waved him into the empty pool room.

"Something wrong?" asked Piney. Mason's hands were shaking, his face pallid.

"Something is fearful wrong. Including me." He leaned against the wall, staring.

"Anything I can do to help?"

Mason groaned. "It's too late."

"Too late for what?" Piney felt the first symptoms of alarm.

"You remember when the offer was made for Razor Edge? And you turned it down, you and Sam?"

"Why, yes. We have no idea of selling."

"I should have warned you then. They made me promise not to tell a soul but I should have told you and Sam."

"Told us what?"

"This company works through El Paso lawyers. They've been buying graze land."

"In the Valley? There's no spare graze left, hasn't been since we came here."

"They've been buying the ranches. Paying extra good prices on condition everybody keep shut about it."

"You mean ranch owners have been selling out? But the Valley is a good place, everyone does well here."

"There's more to it than that. They've been getting threats. If they don't sell they'll be alone and this big company will be against them. They could be ruined in a range war."

"And they all gave in? They all were scared?"

"Every single small rancher in the Valley has sold out but you and Sam. Oh, I should have warned you. I made a commission on every sale, I was greedy. I never felt so guilty in my life."

Piney considered. "I don't know how it would have changed anything, Tom. Sam wouldn't give in to a threat, you know that."

"Maybe not. But you should have known about it. The water, maybe you could have done something about it."

"We have the agreement on the water. The courts will back us on that."

"Piney, when a big company moves in like this, under cover, they'll take the water first, then let you argue it out in the courts. You don't know how it can be in the west when the big men begin to grab."

"I've heard. And I've read some history." He knew that Mason was right. Things had been going so well it was simply impossible for him to grasp that trouble lay ahead. Clancy had been busier than a rooster in a henhouse, the calves had exceeded their highest expectation. There were two other bulls and some Herefords. They had barely broken even, including the income from the barber shop but after the roundup they would be solidly established, with cash ahead. Piney had spent the long weekends living his dream, learning the business, learning the tricks of the trade under Jack Delaney and Sam. His strong, steady barber hands had proven useful; he had mastered the knack of most chores with ease. No one could have been happier.

Mason said, "I'm going home, Piney. I don't feel well. I'm

going to try and think of something. I don't know what, but I'll try."

"Don't make yourself sick. We'll handle it." He knew that Mason was not entirely well, that the boy Tommy inherited a weakness of the lungs which had sent them to this high country. He felt sorry for the land developer, not the strongest character in Quesada but a well-meaning, honest man. He sat in the barber chair and plunged into thought, remembering the good things of the year—and remembering a warning from Sam when he refused to have any traffic with revolvers, believing that nothing but trouble came from owning a short gun.

"Yep, plenty trouble for a sixgun in the hands of drunks and killers," Sam had said. "But also and besides, worse trouble for the galoot who didn't have one handy when said drunks or killers got into action. By the time you get that rifle unlimbered some bum could have you full of hunks of lead, you ever think of that?"

So Piney had practised with the sixgun although he still did not own one, Quesada being such a peaceful town. Now trouble had fallen like a rock on the Valley and he had a problem adjusting to Mason's bad news. Further, he knew how Sam would accept the situation, there was no question of that. Sam would hit the ceiling, then he would begin oiling his guns. There were no odds that Sam would not try to hold Razor Edge in a fight. His stake was too high to quibble, higher than Piney's stake.

During the year the romance between Alicia Maylan and Sam Booker had started Valley heads nodding and smiling. It had not taken more than a few meetings to start the flame. Alicia did not ride in the hills with Ricco any longer; she rode with Sam whenever he could spare the time.

There was no woman for Piney. There were ladies of color in the houses of Silver City and Santa Rita who satisfied his needs, that was no problem. But in his wildest dreams he had never thought of finding a wife in the Valley. And if he envied Sam he concealed the fact in the deepest recesses of his being.

Alicia treated him as one of the family. It was her example which had opened certain doors to him. He worshipped her in a spiritual fashion which he carefully concealed beneath a half-teasing avuncular attitude. In his mind there would be a time when she married Sam and they would all be together on Razor Edge, a happy family. This was the apex of his dreaming, this was all he dared allow himself to want.

To be a black man in New Mexico was better than dwelling in New York but it was not heaven. There was no heaven for him in the world, he thought, just a sort of vestibule where he might be welcome to look on and enjoy the happiness of others. It was the way things were and he was not a rebel. He was, he considered, fortunate. When things were running well and some cash accrued he thought he might take a trip back east and find a woman of his color.

But each time his mind wandered in that direction the vision of Alicia Maylan interfered. His instinct at this moment was to go to the Maylans with Mason's story. He thought about it for several minutes. Maylan, after all, was the law in the Valley. Sam would receive the news better from Alicia than from Piney. He slid down from the chair, a heavy lump in his middle. The clear sky seemed wrong, there should have been clouds, he thought.

The two riders came in from the east. The morning sun threw their shadows ahead of them so that they seemed elongated, tremendous, threatening by their very bulk. They came too swiftly as though bent upon conquest. They were dusty and unshaven but their clothing was tailormade, severe gray in color and they were armed to the teeth. They looked right and left, disdainfully, as the people of Quesada stared, and little Tommy Mason rolled his hoop before them in the innocence of childhood.

In an instant Piney saw that Tommy, concentrating on controlling the erratic behavior of the hoop, was not aware of the riders, nor they of the boy. They were coming too fast and Tommy's hoop wobbled so that he was directly in their path.

Peering from his office window the boy's father yelled, ran for the door. In his excitement he could not turn the knob. A woman screamed and little Tommy suddenly aware of danger looked up and froze, unable to determine which way to run.

Piney came off the curb at full speed. He seized Tommy in one hand, jerking him from under the hoofs of a horse, sending him clear and to the walk where willing hands caught and held him. The horse reared and struck Piney a glancing blow so that he fell and rolled in the dust of the street. His heart beat with trip hammer effect. He lay there, staring up at the amused face of Lige Tinsley.

"Nice goin', nigger," said Tinsley. "Wouldn't want to hurt the boy."

"You damn fool you might have killed him," Piney said, choking in the dust.

Tinsley turned red, his hand streaked to his gun. "Nigger, don't you ever talk thataway to me!"

John Stang reined his big black between them. "Now, Lige. Take it easy. You got to live here!"

"I don't have to take back talk from a nigger!"

"The boy's excited." Stang addressed Piney. "That was a good, quick move you made, boy. Here, take this and go about your business."

Piney stared at a proffered silver dollar. He arose and dusted his clothing. He said, "Keep your money."

"Don't be uppity," said Stang. "Lige won't hurt you. No harm done. Take the cartwheel and buy yourself somethin'."

Before Piney could reply Zeke Maylan's voice cut through. "That'll do, John. Go about your business and leave the man alone. He's a friend of mine."

Stang's head swiveled to regard the Marshal. "Hello, Zeke. Been a long time."

"Not too long. My memory is good."

"Why, Zeke, no sense bein' mad at us. We're goin' to be neighbors here."

"That I won't look forward to," Maylan told him. Alicia came from the store and stood at his side. Tinsley spurred his horse to get a better look. Piney felt the sunshine go out of the day, out of the Valley. Tom Mason had sent his son into the office and was standing, pale and shaken, waiting to be addressed.

Stang said, "Ask your man, there, Mr. Mason. Kay Cross bought in, Zeke."

Tinsley said suddenly, "And this nigger must be partners with Sam Booker. Right?"

"I be damn, I bet you are right," said Stang. He looked down at Piney. "Sure enough?"

"He's Sam's partner," said Maylan. "And a damn sight better man than either of you highbinders. Who'd you buy out?"

"Ask Mr. Mason." Stang was smilingly triumphant. "Meet me over at the hotel, Zeke, we'll talk some."

He waved a hand and Tinsley rode with him to the hitching rack in front of the hotel. They tied up and went up the steps, big men, swaggering and confident. Tinsley cast one long glance back and Piney knew it was for Alicia.

Mason said, "I didn't know it was Kay Cross. I didn't know who it was."

"You mean they bought out the Valley? It was them made the offer to Sam and Piney?" Utter concern was in the Marshal's voice.

"That's it."

Alicia asked, "They bought every ranch?"

"All the graze except Razor Edge."

"It's a grab," said Maylan. "I know those two. I knew them when Tinsley was a button. They let nothin' stand in their way."

"The water," said Alicia. "They'll cut off the water."

"You better go after a court injunction right now," Maylan said to Piney. "Only way to stop 'em. I've got friends in Santa Fe. I'll send a telegraph wire right now."

Mason said again, "I had no way of knowing. They demanded secrecy. I—I'm sorry."

The Marshal gave him a long stare. "We've been friends a long time, Tom. Kay Cross or no, you might have given warning."

"They made me promise. I mean, their lawyers. It was a condition of the sale."

"And you collected commissions."

"Business has been bad, everything was sold out in the Valley, no new people were coming in . . ." Mason's voice trailed off. He said to Piney, "I thank you for what you did. If you knew how I feel now." He turned and went into his office and closed the door behind him.

Alicia said, "Sam doesn't know."

"And I better start things in Santa Fe before he finds out," said Maylan. "There'll be hell to pay, no question about it."

Alicia said, "I'd better ride out and tell Sam."

"Yes," said Piney. "You do that."

"Poor Sam. It'll tear him apart."

"Tell him I'm with him. Whatever happens, he's to make the decisions," said Piney.

"No. You should make them together," she said. "Sam is impetuous. You have more common sense, Piney. I'll tell him he must talk it over with you and papa."

"Whatever you say, Lishia." He watched her go toward the livery stable. He went inside the barber shop and sat in the chair facing the mirror. He held his hands out in front of him. He was shivering inside, but the barber hands were steady through long training, through the thousands of times he had held a razor over a customer's jugular vein without trembling. He knew now what it meant to be raised to a pinnacle of happiness and thrown down in an hour.

After awhile he drew the shade at the window and put out a "Closed for an Hour" sign. He went into the bath house and undressed. He got into a hot tub and washed the dust of Main Street from himself—but he could not wash off the indignity which had been laid upon him before the people of Quesada.

He dressed in range clothing and went back and again looked into the mirror. He was dark brown, not black. His hair was curly but not kinky. His father had told him that he was truly a Talcott, that his grandmother had been impregnated by the owner of the plantation, which was why his father had gained his status as freedman. He had never thought about that one way or the other, it was a matter too common to take into consideration. His own mother had been black, a handsome *bluegum* woman from a tintype now in his possession. Not until this moment had it occurred to him to truly lament the fact of his color. Had he been white Lige Tinsley would never have dared to talk to him as he did in front of all those people—and Alicia Maylan.

He went to the rack where he kept his rifle and a shotgun and where a Colt .45 lay wrapped in an oil cloth. He stared at the weapons for a long while. He had heard many a tale of call out, shoot out from Sam and from the Marshal, stories of other days. What if he sent a message to Tinsley, challenging him?

Tinsley would laugh. He would threaten a whipping. He would never deign to accept the gauge of battle with a Negro. There was no recourse.

A tapping came at the back door. He drew a deep breath and admitted Sam Booker.

"The bastards. The dirty bastards." Sam's voice was thick.

To his dismay Piney felt tears on his cheeks. "They made me feel like a nigger, Sam."

"They'll pay for it."

"It's a long time, too long, since anyone made me feel inferior, black, an animal. Not since I was a little boy in New York among the Irish."

"Tinsley and Stang," said Sam. "Damn their souls to hell."

"You know them too?"

"I know them. They had a foreman name of Jolsen. A rotten skunk. He tried whippin' a kid I knew."

"You stopped him?"

"I shot him."

"I'd like to shoot Tinsley. I truly would." He dabbed at his tears. "Alicia told you about Kay Cross?"

"I met her on the way in. It's pure hell, this thing."

"The Marshal's wiring Santa Fe."

"I know. What can they do, send the militia?" Sam was discouraged, it was evident. "They got a herd outside of town, where we camped on the way in. A thousand head. That's just for starters, Piney. They got gunnies. I can name 'em. Jake Masters, he took Jolsen's place as foreman. Dutch Herman, a butcher. Jose California, a dude with a fast gun. Cooky Harris, he did time in Yuma and lived, he's that tough. Oh, I know Kay Cross. All Texas knows Kay Cross."

"They made the offer to buy us out."

"And we turned it down."

"But you wouldn't sell, leave the Valley?"

"Did I know it was Kay Cross. I'd have thought a heap before refusin'."

"Maybe they'll make another offer. Would you sell?"

"In a minute. We could take our stake and start elsewhere. Further north, Lincoln County, anywhere." He paused, stared at Piney, said apologetically, "I wouldn't of thought that way a year ago. But now—well, with Alicia and all, it's different. Plenty different."

"Well, then." He heaved a sigh from his boots. "If they'll buy let's sell and you can ask Alicia to go along with us."

"Piney, they won't offer. If they do it'll be peanuts, nothin' we could accept. They got us. All they do is build a dam, cut off our water and we're finished."

"But the agreement . . . Santa Fe."

"Like I say, before the courts act we are finished. No, we can do one of two things. We can drive the cattle north and leave the ranch to them. Or we can fight."

"But you don't believe we can beat them in a fight."

"A man can die tryin'. A year ago that wouldn't cut any ice with me. But now—it's like I say. Alicia."

"And we can't move out—run."

"We can. But if we did every son in the west with a wide loop would be hauntin' us. Word gets around. Run once and you got the mark on you."

The depth of Sam's dolor had an odd effect. Piney felt the need to bolster his partner. He remembered the man Tinsley staring hard at Alicia with his bold eyes and all his protective instinct arose.

He said, "Sam, let me give you a haircut and a shave. Then you can clean up and we'll go over to Maylan's and study some more on it."

"If we could hire some gunslingers I know," Sam muttered. "But then we'd be gettin' the whole Valley into a war. It'll take a lot more'n studyin' on it, Piney, a whole hell of a lot more."

In the hotel bar where Amos Jones, proprietor, maintained the exclusive atmosphere for the more important people of the Valley, Stang and Tinsley sat at a corner table and spoke in low voices. Jones instinctively kept his distance, recognizing power and danger, not daring to eavesdrop.

Stang said, "It'll work out fine."

"Why shouldn't it?" Tinsley grinned. "We took our time and made sure of everything."

"People are like broncos. Some you can gentle right easy. Others, you got to take a club to get their attention."

"Like Booker and his nigger."

"Better take it easy on the nigra."

"Nigger. He's an uppity black bastard, rotten spoiled."

"He's the town nigra. We got to live with the town."

"We try to live with the town. First off we got to cut Razor Edge off of water. That'll rile people. Then what?"

"We spend a little," said Stang. "The farmers won't fight. The town people can be bought, I've found. They're all for business. We give 'em business."

"We drive that herd through town tomorrow and they'll sit up and pay attention."

"We drive that herd around town. They'll know. We make a big talk about how we wouldn't inconvenience the good people. The worst thing we can do is stir 'em up now. It was bad about Mason's boy."

"I never saw that brat. I was lookin' at the Marshal's

daughter. She just came out of the store and she is sure somethin' to look at."

"None of that, now," said Stang quickly. "That's the very worst. You mess with Zeke Maylan's daughter and it will be the last woman you fool around with."

"I ain't thinkin' of messin' around." Tinsley sipped his whiskey. "You want me to take charge here, don't you? Live here awhile?"

"That's the idea."

"I done my messin' around. I'm thinkin' of marryin' and raisin' a family."

"Zeke won't cotton to the notion, I'm warnin' you."

"You keep warnin' me about that old coot. John, there's ways and ways. I got a way with the gals, you might have noticed. Let me get to her and the old man'll come around."

"You better not bet on that."

"That gal's got quality. She's a lady, anybody can see it. That's what I want in a wife. And when I go for a woman I get her. You watch me."

"It means you got to change your ways a heap," Stang warned. "I dunno if you're up to it. You got to walk straight if you want to get along with people like the Maylans. I know Zeke."

"What's so special about him, anyhow?"

"He's honest but he's more. He'll shoot your eye out if you corner him. He was a hiyu man in the old cowtowns. You was too young to know. He was what the big name fellas thought they was. He made Masterson and Earp and them look small."

"That was another time."

"Zeke's about my age," said Stang quietly.

"Well . . . I'm goin' to make a try at the daughter anyhow. Never saw a woman took my fancy on sight like that."

"Walk easy," said Stang. "And look out for Sam Booker."

"I haven't forgot him."

"You remember what he done to Jolsen."

"Jolsen was drunk."

"He gave Jolsen first shot."

"Booker ain't that fast. I'm quicker."

"Quick ain't everything. A man like Booker, he can be cold. He's killed plenty. Thing is, I'm kinda countin' on that side of him."

"Like how?"

"Like you push him, he'll explode. He'll start a fight. People can be made to believe he's the one began a war—if we got to have a war with Razor Edge."

"Some war. That little outfit against ours."

"Any war is a somethin'," said John Stang. "We come in here, we're outlanders. We can't run wild without we got somethin' on our side. Bad enough we're goin' to build the dam. Only way we can make that work, we give water to the farmers, keep them quiet. We only cut off Razor Edge. Don't make no mistake, Lige. Politics is important."

"Oh, I know. You convinced me."

"And the nigra."

"I got to admit you make plenty of sense," said Tinsley.

"He's the barber. You patronize his shop. You treat him decent."

"I won't kowtow to no black sonofabitch."

"You treat him like you would anybody else," said Stang. "I'm goin' to stay right here for awhile. I'm goin' to know what's happenin' until things settle down. You listen to what I tell you, Lige, this here is new country and the less trouble the better."

"I know you're right." Tinsley moved restlessly. "I can't go against you, John."

CHAPTER FOUR

Upon the hill behind the ranch house at Razor Edge Sam Booker held field glasses on the herd winding and spreading over the ranches of the valley. Earlier he had seen his neighbors move out in a melange of wagons, lock, stock and barrel. Their cattle remained, Kay Cross had bought all the stock, it seemed. Alicia Maylan and Ricco Camponetta moved uneasily without talk. The very size of the herd, the riders with their rifles, the wagons carrying supplies, the pall of dust over everything stifled them to silence.

Sam said, "Well, what do you know? Joe Beasley. They sobered him up and put him on a horse."

"It's his chance to get even with you and Jack," said Ricco. "He's been making threats all year."

"I wish they were all Beasleys," said Sam.

"You're goin' to fight them?"

"I am. You're not," Sam told the young man. "You're fired."

"No go," said Ricco. "You fight—I fight. I work for Razor Edge. I couldn't hold up my head if I quit."

Alicia said, "You can't win, Sam. Kay Cross is too big."

"Look, I'm not startin' anything against Kay Cross. I'm not about to make a move until they do. But Ricco saw a gang of workmen up on Little Bear. They weren't building houses. They were building a dam."

"They'll kill you, Sam."

"I don't know. Piney said last night that they might stop at killin' people. The Marshal's already wired a message to Santa Fe protesting."

"Sam, you know there'll be raiding and shooting."

"Bound to be some."

"Those men you pointed out to us, they're all badmen."

"Stang didn't bring any other kind. But we can't prove anything until they start up."

Ricco said, "They'll start. And we'll start right back. Remember, Sam, I know these hills, I know this country. I know some people in town who won't hold still for this."

"Your father and Zeke and who else?"

"I know them," he said doggedly. "Now I better go help Delaney. He's got four farm kids and a couple saddle bums and he's about loco."

"I should be down there," said Sam dully.

"No. You leave it to us. We're about finished, got the calves branded, the herd ready to put in the home pasture." Ricco slid down the hill without waiting for an answer. He was riding Big Red, his favorite stallion. He vanished in the direction of the Razor Edge herd.

The procession of Kay Cross beef and power was about over. Beasley was part of the drag. Sam put down the field glasses he had long ago bought from an army sergeant who had stolen them from an officer. Alicia sat close to him.

Sam said, "I was goin' to ask you for real last night."

"You don't have to ask, darling."

"I was goin' to talk to Zeke about us."

"He knows."

"It's no good now, Lishia."
"Why not?"
"I can't let you get mixed up in this."
"You don't think I'm not mixed up in it?"
"You can stay clear. There's nothing in the world that would make me let you be in it. This'll be a war, no two ways about it. A bad, nasty war."
"You'll need all the help you can get."
"Not from you."
"From me most of all. If you feel as you say you do, as I believe you do."
"Lishia, you don't know what it means."
"I'm Zeke Maylan's daughter," she told him. "What I haven't seen I've heard about. I'm a western woman, Sam."
"I won't marry you and make you a widow."
She said, "Sam, you don't have to marry me. You don't have to do anything about me. I'm here and I'll be here."
He turned toward her and she fell against him. They sat with their arms around each other. He had no way to tell her that it wouldn't work, that it was all wrong. She had defeated him, he could not reject her. He loved her as he had never believed he could love anyone or anything.
After a long while she rearranged her clothing and asked, "Are you convinced now, darling?"
"I'm convinced but I'm scared."
"Let's go back to town for the night. Delaney and Ricco can manage. I don't want you out of my sight until we can talk things over with papa and Piney."
"I ought to be out there."
"Not in your frame of mind. Please, Sam."
He agreed reluctantly. Life had suddenly become terrifically complicated. He was in love and inside him a fire had started fed with the fuel of growing hatred of Kay Cross and all for which it stood.

Over the twelve months Piney Talcott's shop had gradually become a meeting place for the men of Quesada. Finnegan and Amos Jones at first resented the desertion of their bars, then found themselves in the habit of joining Joe Parker, the banker, and Casper, the carpenter, and Tom Mason and others in the slack hours of late afternoon. They read the week old Santa Fe papers and El Paso papers and the more ancient Police Gazette and Leslie's and discussed various and sundry topics at great length. Their talk was always larded by Piney's few but salty commentaries, they had accepted him fully. Only Otto Mueller and a few others remained aloof.

On this anniversary day the talk was of Kay Cross and what it meant. Lars Larsen, a successful farmer, was worried about fence. Everyone knew the precarious situation of Razor Edge but this they did not openly discuss. The general opinion was that business would be better in the Valley if Kay Cross operated on a fair play basis.

The door of the shop opened and Lige Tinsley entered. He was dressed in town clothing, obviously tailor made, shiny boots and a Stetson hat. He was smiling.

"Gentlemen. Name's Tinsley. I aim to be in town quite a while."

They announced their names to him. He shook hands with each, looking directly into their eyes, still smiling. Piney stood beside his chair expressionless, watching the man, estimating him, his strength, his potential.

Tinsley said, "Mr. Talcott, I need a haircut and a shave. Am I next?"

"You are, sir," said Piney. He placed a clean towel about the neck of the big man, lowered the chair. "Do you like your hair close or medium?"

"Medium. But a close shave, I like it real close." He surveyed the silent, staring men of Quesada. "Mason, I'm sorry what happened with your boy. Got a little present for him, I'll send it over tomorrow. A Barlow. Nothin' like a real Barlow jacknife for a growin' boy. Okay?"

"Tommy doesn't play with knives," said Mason stiffly.

"Well, when he grows up to it, eh?" He settled himself comfortably in the chair and raised his voice a trifle over the metallic snip of Piney's shears. "Guess everybody's wonderin' about Kay Cross. Well, I can tell you anything you want to know. It's all right good for the town, that's for starters."

"Ya, but what about da farmers?" asked Larsen.

"Fine, you'll be fine. We'll be ridin' our fence, keepin' the law. Kay Cross wants no trouble with anybody."

A dangerous man, thought Piney. The violence in him had been plain when he had nearly run down Tommy Mason. Now he was displaying another facet, he was politicking, attempting to blunt the danger from any outfit as huge as Kay Cross, playing to the various factions, lining them up.

"Yep, and we'll do all our buyin' in town," Tinsley said. "The railway will be to Silver City in a month but we figure to buy here, ship from there. That means prosperity for Quesada, don't it?"

"Could be," said Joe Parker. "You haven't deposited in the bank yet."

"That'll come in time. This here will be an independent operation. As we profit, we bank with you. We been thinkin' on it for a year, you know."

"Buyin' up the ranches," said Parker.

"That was good business. Once it got out a big concern was buyin' the prices would go up, you know that. We paid good as it was." He spoke to Piney, his voice a bit sharp. "We offered you a good price, didn't we, Talcott?"

"It didn't seem enough to us," said Piney. He was working with great care and deliberation. He knew fear of this man, he sensed the power of evil in him; it was strong enough to make him catch his breath.

"Sorry," said Tinsley. "Would you sell now?"

"Best you should talk to my partner," Piney said.

"We can only offer you about half of the first deal," said Tinsley carelessly. "We're satisfied with what we got. Of course in a year or so we'll need more graze."

"And by then you'll have us cut out," said Piney without heat. "That's good business too, right?"

Tinsley did not speak for a moment. Everyone in the shop held his breath. The shears snipped and snipped, a bright clatter in the stillness.

Then Tinsley addressed the assembled men of Quesada. "You heard him. I didn't say that. We ain't makin' any threats against anybody in this here Valley. We aim to be peaceable."

Finnegan said, "So long as your men are peaceable in my place, well, what can I do but serve 'em? Nothin' to me who drinks my booze."

"Ahem," said Amos Jones. "Your patronage of my hotel is appreciated. What else is there to say?"

"Nothin', not a word," said Tinsley. "We'll all get along snug as bugs in a rug."

Finnegan said, "Yeah . . . well . . . Better be gettin' back to business." He left.

One by one the others drifted away. Piney concluded the haircut, held up a mirror. He was not surprised at the departure of the men who had been his friends. He and Sam were set apart now, the promise of new business, bigger profits did not extend to them. Power had manifested itself in honeyed terms, there was no ground upon which to fight it so far as the citizenry was concerned. The farmers were safe beyond the fence, the merchants would make more money, why should they complain?

Tinsley broke in upon his thoughts. "You see how quick they run, *Mister* Talcott?"

"They're human beings."

"They're suckers. You'll learn about people before this hullabaloo is over. People are all chickenshit."

"That's your opinion, Mr. Tinsley." He again held up the mirror. "Is your haircut satisfactory?"

"It'll do." He resettled himself as Piney lowered the chair to the reclining position in preparation for the shave. "You're some kind of educated nigra, ain't you?"

"In a fashion. I went to school. Since then it's been experience that taught me certain things."

"Must say I never met one like you."

Piney applied lather to the strong, heavy beard. "I've met a lot like you, Mr. Tinsley."

"Why, most everybody's like me, boy. I mean—Mister Talcott, gotta remember you're the town's nigra."

Piney was stropping the razor. His blood congealed, he had to force himself to remain calm. "This is not Texas."

"You betcha it ain't. Kay Cross is bringin' Texas to this country. Ha!" He was pleased with his fancy.

Piney poised the sharp blade. "And no man is worthy of your trust? All are evil?"

"Just about."

Piney began shaving the cheek. "It's odd you should say that."

"Why shouldn't I if I believe it?" He was caught in the dialogue with a black man, vaguely resenting it but unable to withdraw with what he considered his dignity.

"Because you do have trust."

"You gotta show me."

Piney twisted the razor so that light reflected from its gleaming surface. He said quietly, "You are right now showing your trust in me."

For one instant he saw that which he wanted to see. The pupils of Tinsley's eyes dilated, the corner of his mouth twitched. The razor lay diagonally across his throat. One slight stroke and he would be nothing but a puff of wind across the Valley of Quesada, a leaf blown past the scene in the wake of a wanton breeze.

"You wouldn't . . . no!" The spark of fear vanished. "Wouldn't get you nothin' but hung."

"We'd be buried together," said Piney. "It is a thought now, isn't it, Mr. Tinsley?"

"No good. It ain't in you." The big body relaxed again.

"Oh, you're quite right. It's not in me to murder. Therefore you trust me because I believe in justice?"

"Nope. You just ain't got the guts."

Piney resumed his task, working with great care and skill. "Mr. Tinsley, you say that. I think you don't quite believe it." He pressed the mouth shut, working all the while. "Whatever Kay Cross does in the Valley I think you'll remember that you did, for a moment, realize that a man has to trust another man at times, under certain circumstances. Yes, I think you'll remember that black is the color of skin but not the color of the innards, not always. And that white men sometimes have black souls."

Tinsley did not dare move his head. He stared upward, fury in his eyes and another emotion. It was respect, perhaps, at least acknowledgment. When Piney continued shaving his neck he neither flinched nor spoke. He accepted the final rites, the hot towel, still silent.

"Do you care for Pinaud's?" Piney asked.

"That's for sissies," said Tinsley. He adjusted his cravat and donned his coat without help from Piney. He went to the doorway, then turned. "Yes, you're an uppity nigger. Shouldn't never be educated, it brings out the bad. Niggers ain't white folks and don't you ever forget it."

"Not a chance," said Piney serenely. "But on occasion—I can feel lucky, can't I?"

For a moment he thought Tinsley was going to attack him. Then the Texan managed a meager smile. "Texas has come to Quesada. You'll learn, Mister Talcott. You'll learn."

He slammed the door behind him. Piney looked at the razor and again he was shaking inside while his hand remained steady as a rock. He washed the blade with extra care, wiped it, stropped it. He had taken the measure of the man and he had found it more than he had expected—hoped. Tinsley was afraid because of the helplessness of his situation, he thought. The man was as dangerous as a human can be, a man steeped in the prejudices and beliefs of the heroes of the cattle business which dominated the Southwest. Grab and keep hold, that was what they held to be proper, even noble. It was not as he had read in the paperbacks and the gazettes.

But then he had known that for some time, since traveling as a Negro through the western country. He had learned many things, as he had suggested to Tinsley. Now he was learning one more lesson, to live with fear, for others as much as for himself. Texas had come to the Valley, the worst of Texas.

The Maylan parlor was roomy, furnished western Southwest style, rawhide settee and chairs, colorful Navajo and Mexican rugs and wall hangings, cushions for comfort covered with Indian designs. Sam Booker sat with his boots extended and stared at nothing.

"I know Kay Cross and Texans like Stang and Tinsley. They think they got special rights."

"I think we should be married," said Alicia.

The Marshal drew on a pipe during the small following silence. Sam's jaw tightened, his hands, big and strong but seeming helpless now, twitched in his lap.

The Marshal said, "I believe with Sam. It ain't the time. Not that we ain't in the trouble to come. We are. But a weddin' wouldn't be fittin', somehow."

"You're wrong, both of you. I want to be in it as Sam's wife. It may have some effect on them. Doesn't Stang have a daughter my age?"

"Two of 'em. Back at school in the East. He ain't got time for daughters. He's got time for Tinsley, his adopted son."

"They think God gave 'em a right," Sam repeated. "The graze is theirs if they can take it and hold it."

"Haven't had a reply from Santa Fe," said the Marshal. "It wouldn't surprise me they got more influence up there than I got."

"You know they have. They buy judges and politicians like sacks of potatoes."

"Trouble is, my friends are honest. They go through the legal processes which are mighty slow."

"But we've started it. In the end we'll get an injunction. New Mexico won't let Texans take over the Valley," urged Alicia.

"John Chisum made himself felt up north. John Slaughter carries weight in Santa Fe," said Sam. "No, we got to fight 'em right here."

"And lose everything."

"They'll make an offer," said Maylan. "You goin' to listen, Sam?"

"Not to their offer, if they make one."

"I see your point."

"But how can we just let them ruin us?" demanded Alicia.

"We don't let 'em," Sam said gently. "We do what we can."

"And die!"

Sam said, "It's the way a man is." It was difficult for him to explain. "He fights for a place. Then he's got to be ready for anything to hold on."

"And a Tinsley comes to town with guns at his beck and call," said Alicia. "It's rotten. It's unfair and rotten."

There was a tap at the door. The Marshal opened and Lige Tinsley stood framed in the lamplight, hat in hand, smiling directly at Alicia.

"Marshal. Thought I might make a duty call, seein's I'm to be a neighbor."

Maylan stepped aside, bound by the rigid rules of western hospitality, displeased but polite. "You know Sam Booker."

"Why, sure. Sam, how are you this evenin'?"

"Poorly, thanks."

"My daughter Alicia," said Maylan without warmth. "Lige Tinsley of Kay Cross."

She said unexpectedly, "How do you do, Mr. Tinsley? Please come in and sit awhile."

He put his hat upon a table and chose a straight chair, sitting with his back erect, glancing from one to the other, never losing his easy smile. Sam gathered his legs beneath him, scenting trouble, instantly aware that the man's interest lay in Alicia. It was obvious that Tinsley had just come from the barber shop and he wondered what had taken place there. He listened to the desultory conversation without joining in, waiting for Tinsley to make a point.

It came soon. Tinsley said, "Glad you're here, Sam. We wondered if you'd reconsider on sellin' Razor Edge."

"At twice what you offered, might do that."

"I was thinkin' about half what we offered. Things is different now. What we'd do is let you keep your stock, drive it to the next place you choose."

"We're shippin' from Silver City right soon," said Sam. "Be a bad time to sell out."

"We'll give you time."

"Until you build the dam?"

Tinsley said, "Figure you'll get an injunction against any dam. Kay Cross knows that."

"I see. But you'll build it."

"Truth is, we need every square foot of graze there is. We don't aim to bother farmers, they're needed. Just the graze. It's purely business, nothin' personal. Kay Cross has got to feed its stock."

"You know somethin', Lige? Razor Edge has got the same problem."

"Reckon that's the truth." Tinsley was cheerful. "Just had a talk with your pardner. He says your word goes."

"We agree."

"He's some pardner. I hear people have him to supper and all in this town."

"He's a friend of ours," said Maylan.

"He's a fine barber, best I ever seen," said Tinsley. He arose and bowed to Alicia. "I'll give myself the pleasure of callin' again if I can."

She said, "That might be nice, Mr. Tinsley."

His eyes lighted. "Mighty nice of you. Marshal. . . . Sam . . ." He stared at Sam. "Only one trouble with your pardner."

"He too much man for you?" Sam blazed, moving his feet again, ready to leap.

"Too much man for his own good," said Tinsley without anger. "Man gets above himself he can find trouble."

"Oh, there'll be trouble," Sam said. "Never did think Kay Cross wouldn't bring trouble. Jolsen was trouble."

"Jolsen drank too much booze," said Tinsley. "Well, this has been a real pleasure. Good night, folks."

They sat for awhile after the door closed. Then Maylan went noiselessly out the back door and walked around the house and came in at the front door. He shook his head.

"The man's too smart to stick around and listen. He's plumb dangerous, Sam."

"Like a snake."

Alicia said, "Worse."

"Yes, Miss," said Sam. "And I notice you was pretty polite to the snake."

"I will go riding with him," she said.

"You'll do what?" demanded her father.

"He's interested," she said.

"You won't do any such of a thing!" said Sam.

"I'll go driving or riding with him. I'll listen to him." She wheeled around, defiant. "You'd fight them with guns and nothing more. You won't marry me until it's over—and then it's six, two and even you'll be a corpse. All right. I'll fight them my way, a woman's way."

"I won't let you!" said the Marshal. "Anything could happen to you."

"What do you think's going to hapen to me if Kay Cross wipes out Razor Edge? And Sam? And Piney—you heard him threaten Piney. You know how easy it is to turn some people against a black man. You're all so wrapped up in being brave, defending your property that you don't see what can happen, you don't realize the terrible danger to everyone, every single soul in the Valley, even those who kowtow to Kay Cross."

"You can't do it!"

"You can't stop me."

"If that skunk puts a hand on you I'll kill him before the sun is down."

"Other men have put hands on me, Sam," she said kindly. "Do you love me less because of that?"

"You know what I mean."

"I won't have it, Lishia. I won't have you messin' around with that lady-killin' no good rattler."

"Just so he rattles first, I can handle him. Or any man."

Marshal Maylan said, "Just a minute, now."

"Don't let her do it," Sam pled.

"No, just a minute. I lived with this gal a long time. She's got more sense 'n I have, sometimes. And she can take care of herself good. She's owned a hideout derringer since she was sixteen. You ain't got a chance, Sam, against Kay Cross, you and Ricco and Delaney. But with her spyin' and maybe influencin' Tinsley a bit—the odds get better."

"I can't see it."

The Marshal got up and went to a peg on the wall and

took down his gunbelt. "For years I been wearin' this because of habit. Could be I'll need it some time soon. You listen to Alicia, believe me, Sam. You listen good. I'll leave it up to her myself." He went to make his stroll through the streets to check the state of law and order in Quesada.

She went swiftly to Sam and kissed him. "You see? Papa trusts me. Don't you trust me, darling?"

"You know I trust you. It's him."

"The lady killer? Don't you know his type are so vain they can't believe every woman isn't ready to fall for them?"

"I know his type real good."

"I'm going to do it, Sam." There was a glint in her eye. "I'm going to try to learn all I can about Kay Cross."

He said glumly, "I ain't altogether a fool. I see there's nothin' I can do to stop you."

She said, "Then kiss me and don't think about it. Let it be played any way it comes from the ace."

There was nothing else he could do, he realized.

CHAPTER FIVE

Marshal Zeke Maylan and his daughter watched John Stang wave to them from the stage en route to El Paso. The town of Quesada was going about its business in the most normal fashion. It was a bright summer day and Tom Mason crossed the street to them.

Mason said, "Well, it does seem like Stang's kept his word. Razor Edge cattle on the way to Silver City, no fences cut, business flourishing in the Valley."

"It does seem so," said the Marshal. He went inside the Wells Fargo office to wait for the mail brought in by the stage to be sorted.

Mason said, "You've been riding out with Lige Tinsley, what do you think, Alicia?"

"So far, so good." She looked at him. "You're not satisfied, are you, Tom?"

"I've never forgiven myself for letting them move in without warning you people. I took my commission without thinking of my friends. No, I'm not convinced. They've never fully stopped work on that dam."

"They've allowed water to the farms. They've built ditches over all the property they bought."

"And they can cut off Razor Edge in a day."

"They can." She added frankly, "Tom, I agree with you. Kay Cross never stops growing—grabbing. Half the people in the Valley agree with you. But if they ever go to sleep Kay Cross will have it all, farms, everything, before they wake up."

"I keep telling them."

"I know you do."

"I'll never forget Piney yanking little Tommy from under Tinsley's horse and Tinsley not caring a thing about it. Wasn't for John Stang I do believe Tinsley would have started a war before now."

"Not quite," she told him. "Not quite but almost."

"Those gunslingers up at their headquarters, they worry me."

"They're on deck to worry people," she said.

"Well, Sam and Ricco and Jack are on their way to Silver City. They'll have capital, cash when they come back. Then we'll see."

"You think Kay Cross is letting them cash in before they close off the water?"

"I wouldn't be surprised," said Mason.

"It could be." Her plan had worked up until now, she thought, rather sadly. Lige had made a big pretense of being on the side of law and order, on her father's side. His courtship had been constant but restrained. He had been insistent that Kay Cross meant to live and let live.

The trouble was that no one believed this. Piney, Sam, her father—and truthfully herself—only waited for the move to be made by the invading Texans. It was becoming more and more difficult for her to stall Tinsley, to evade his proposals. And Sam was growing more and more impatient with her consorting with the Kay Cross man.

Her father was worried, the town was gossiping and Sam was getting jealous. Still, she felt she had caused Tinsley to delay punitive action against Razor Edge. Only Piney believed that she was doing the right thing; it had been Piney's private support which had enabled her to continue to keep Tinsley dangling. Now it was all coming to a head and she felt uncomfortable in her position as lady spy. Sam was due back in a day or two and she would talk with him, she promised herself. If he once more asked her to stop seeing Tinsley she would do so.

Mason was saying, "Say, looks like Zeke has good news!"

Her father came from the Wells Fargo office waving a long, official looking envelope. "We got it, we got it!"

"From Santa Fe?"

"Judge Earle granted an injunction against a dam cutting off the water supply to anyone previously settled in the Valley!"

She sighed in deep relief. "Thank goodness!"

Mason said, "That'll tear it. Piney! Hey, Piney!"

Piney came from the barbershop. They walked to him and now other people on the street paused and the news spread like wildfire through the town. A farmer cracked his whip and drove his team out to tell the farmers in the outlying area.

Piney said, "It's great news. But it could start trouble, couldn't it?"

"Kay Cross has said again and again it won't go against the law," said Maylan. "I'm saddlin' up right now to ride out and serve notice on Tinsley."

"I'll go with you," said Alicia.

"You will not," said her father.

"You should have a deputy," suggested Mason. "You know those gunslingers, you've had trouble with them every time they came to town."

"No real trouble," said the Marshal. "I've handled that kind before."

"That Dutch Herman is a dumb ox," said Mason. "I don't trust those men."

"Tinsley can handle them. No, this is my job. It'll be a real pleasure," said the Marshal. He walked rapidly toward the livery stable.

"There's no talking to him when he's in this mood," Alicia told the two who looked anxiously after. "But he's right. Lige wouldn't let anything happen to him."

"That's right," said Piney. "Kay Cross will want to think it over. Stang'll have to be notified." He stopped, smacked his hands together. "Say, we've got to send a telegram to Sam right now. He should know the good news."

"Right," said Alicia. She took his arm. "Let's do it right now."

They went into the Wells Fargo telegraph-office-post-office together.

Marshal Maylan passed farm wagons, an occasional horseman on the road westward, greeting them with a wave. It was the hour after the noon sun had reached high position and the land lay bright but without the purple shadows of the high plain that he had learned to love. The Kay Cross was headquartering at the old Payson place several miles past Razor Edge. He was in no hurry, savoring the pleasure of serving the injunction upon Tinsley.

It was wrong to gloat over performing a legal duty, he thought, but he had disliked Lige Tinsley on sight. He knew about John Stang and others of his kind and was resigned to their greed and ruthlessness. Tinsley was another matter, narrow-eyed, too handsome, swaggering in a sneering, superior way, always chasing a woman. Chasing Alicia, he added, his resentment growing.

He knew better than to try and rein in on Alicia when her mind was made up. She took after her dead mother; she could not be bullied. And, he supposed, she took after her father in many ways. She was certainly unafraid, even of a man like Tinsley. She was in love with Sam Booker and that was another matter.

Sam was behaving perfectly in the Valley but Sam had a past and the Marshal knew about men like him, also. In fact there was no sort of man in the west that Zeke Maylan had not encountered and observed. His career had been thorough and it spanned the swift history of the cow trails and those who operated in the cattle trade and around its fringes. Sam could be as dangerous as Lige Tinsley. What he lacked was the scheming mind of a John Stang. Sam would never make it big, he would be a rancher and dwell in the Valley and with any kind of luck manage to get along with Kay Cross until it moved on.

If Kay Cross moved on, that was. If the grama grass died in a bad season the big outfit would move to pastures literally greener. If the graze held Sam would have Kay Cross on his back and that boded no good for Razor Edge —which included Alicia.

This injunction was a stopgap, Maylan ruminated. Once

it was served Kay Cross would not openly violate it for fear of repercussions from Santa Fe, a possible callout of the militia, interference with other Stang-Tinsley projects. But there would be attempts to have it set aside, searches for crooked legislators and judges already open to bribery, all kinds of moves. Sam being the kind of man he was, Kay Cross would have to move him out sooner or later.

The best thing Sam could do would be to take the money he received for the herd, round up Clancy and the other bull and some cows and head for another graze. If possible he would talk Sam into this. He had a few dollars saved for Alicia when she married, maybe that would sway them—both the girl and Sam. Although he doubted this . . .

He came to the road leading to the Payson ranch and reined onto it. He was riding a big sorrel which liked to run uphill, a strange animal but one with a nice, rolling gait. The Kay Cross men would be busy with the finishing touches of their roundup which necessarily took longer than that of Razor Edge with a smaller herd, he thought, but Tinsley was reasonably certain to be at the house with the final paperwork. It would be right nice to see the man's face when the injunction was presented to him.

He dismounted, opened a fence gate, led the sorrel through, closed the gate behind him. The house was atop a hill like most of those in the Valley. He rode into the yard and called out and Joe Beasley appeared from behind the nearby barn. Dutch Herman was close behind, a pint bottle of whiskey in his hand, his round, empty face thick with stupidity.

Beasley grabbed a shotgun from a post of the corral. Already dismounted, Maylan wished he was back in the saddle for greater mobility against these two oafs. If his eyes had been as sharp as they used to be, he would have perceived that they were drunk and acted accordingly. Now he was in a crossfire and it had been a long time and his age was against him.

Out of his experience he used a sharp, peremptory tone. "Joe . . . Dutch . . . I'm here to see Lige. He around?"

Beasley said, "He wants t' see Lige. You get that, Dutch?"

"Yah. Lige, he ain't here right now." Dutch swigged from the bottle but his right hand remained on his gun butt.

"Y' hear that? Spyin' around, huh, Marshal? You and Booker and the nigger, all spies."

Maylan said, "Where is Lige?"

"None o' your damn business." Beasley had the shotgun half-raised. "You nor none of your podners is wanted here. Get it? Not wanted. Right, Dutch?"

"Right," said Dutch. "Spyin' around."

"And his goddam hoor daughter," said Beasley, "spyin'."

Maylan said, "What was that, Beasley? I didn't hear that, did I?"

The shotgun's twin muzzles rose higher, centered on Maylan's middle. "Ha! You heard it. I said it, din't I? Goddam hoor daughter."

Maylan said, "One more chance, Joe. Put down that shotgun."

Now he was not making sense and he knew it down deep but he was not living down deep at the moment. He was seeing red in a situation wherein he should be cool and calm. All the years of his service he had remained in possession of all his faculties. Now it was gone in the face of that shotgun and the two ignorant slobs who faced him. There was more to this, he thought fleetingly, than appeared on the surface. There was more belligerency in these two, more animosity, more desire to goad him than seemed proper. He should wait and temporize and try to learn something but the reference to Alicia made it impossible.

He was wearing a coat. The injunction was in the breast pocket. The skirt of the coat brushed the butt of his sixgun. He began to move his right hand as though to adjust his vest.

Beasley said, "What'd Lige tell us this mornin' when we was havin' the confab? Wha'd he say?"

"Keep that stinkin' lawman out of it. Keep him away," said Dutch Herman. "He could roon the whole idee."

"That's what he said."

Maylan seized upon the switch of subject. "What idea? What did Lige mean by that? Answer me!"

"Answer him," said Beasley. "The skunk, the lousy lawman servin' papers on ev'body, takin' a man's ranch away."

"You're an ignorant damned fool, Joe," said Maylan. "And you're makin' a hell of a mistake. Put down that gun!"

"I'll shove it down your damn throat!"

Now Maylan knew, because of his past, because of his experience, that Beasley meant to do what he said. He meant to fire buckshot down his throat. He was drunk enough to do that and there was some other reason, some new reason. The only possible defense was to move to the right, draw with his right hand and hope he could take only part of the charge, hope it wasn't buckshot but birdshot against encroaching crows, hope Dutch Herman wasn't sober enough to take advantage of the situation, hope Lige Tinsley was somewhere within hearing, hope a hundred different things. He moved.

Beasley yelled, "You lawman bastard," and fired the shotgun.

Maylan went down to one knee. The blast was hot and he knew it was buck. He laid the Colt level and fired once. Beasley went backwards as though jerked by a rope. The shotgun flew from his hands. Maylan swung his Colt to cover Dutch Herman.

Dutch Herman already had his gun in his hand. He howled, "You kilt Joe awready," and fired twice.

The first shot caught Maylan in the right shoulder and forced him to drop the revolver. He had a moment when he scrabbled with his left hand, twisted, turning under the force of the .45 bullet, his eyes shaded by the shock. He lay half-sprawled, seeking the gun. The second shot took him in the head and then he knew only that he was dropping, dropping down a great well and that he would never fight again nor see his daughter nor know what happened in the Valley. It was a sort of regret that he felt without pain, just a sense of loss, a slipping away and out, a journey to be undertaken from which there was no return. . . .

Lige Tinsley, riding in from the near herd where he had been making a last tally, heard the shots and came fast with gun drawn. He rounded the corral and saw Beasley stretched flat, arms spread wide and beyond Beasley he saw Maylan on his side, half his skull blown away. He saw the Colt in Dutch Herman's hand and swung a blow with the back of his right clenched hand that sent Dutch reeling, then came down from the saddle and wrenched the revolver away and struck the big man again.

"You goddam fool, what the hell is all this?" he demanded.

"He kilt Joe," babbled Dutch Herman. "He'd of kilt me."

Jake Masters, lean and sardonic, rode into the scene. He jumped to earth and examined first Beasley then Maylan.

Tinsley slapped the whiskey bottle from Dutch's hand with the muzzle of the revolver.

"Deader'n mackerels," said Masters. He picked up the shotgun. "Joe musta missed with this. Maylan made a good move and got him. See the marks in the dirt? Then Dutch pulled down from over yonder."

Tinsley broke the Colt. "Shot him twice."

"Right," said Masters. "Thing is, what started it?"

Tinsley walked to Maylan's side, then knelt and saw the edge of the long, official envelope protruding from the coat pocket. He extracted it, read the contents.

"I be damned," he said. He arose, stared at Dutch. "What started it. Don't lie to me or I'll turn you in and have you hanged for murder."

"Uh—yah. Joe, he started callin' names. Like you told us, eh? The Marshal could spoil it? This mornin'?"

"Oh you goddam fools," said Tinsley. "Oh you frightenin' damn fools."

"Vell, Joe, you know how he was. About the ranch, eh?'

"You mean he wanted to shoot Maylan, don't you?"

"Vell . . . he called the gal a hoor," said Dutch. "That I did not believe, she rides with you, sure, but no hoor, eh?"

"He called Alicia a whore?"

"Vunce, tvice. The Marshal, he was crazy mad, eh?"

Tinsley tapped the injunction against his teeth. He was furious yet he was thinking hard. He could have killed Herman on the spot, he could still turn him in to the people of Quesada as the murderer of the Marshal. On the other hand . . .

He said to Masters, "You and Dutch bury that dumb drunk."

"Beasley? What about Maylan?"

"Put him in the barn under a blanket. I got to figure things out."

"How about the other thing? It is on?"

"I got to figure, I tell you. Bury that carcass where it won't be found. Take it into the hills."

"Can I get some help?"

Tinsley looked hard at him. "No. I don't want anybody to know." He started for the house and Masters followed until they were out of earshot of the still dazed Dutch Herman. He said, "You know we can't trust that dumb

Dutchman. But don't kill him now. Just keep him from blabbin'. You got the watch on the road from Silver City?"

"Jose and Cooky are both on the job."

"If anybody else asks, tell 'em Beasley pulled stakes."

"Sure. We got time. Four, five hours mebbe."

"I got to think."

"Yeah. Killin' Maylan, that was the dumbest thing could happen right now."

"We got to turn it around," said Tinsley. "We got to make it work for us."

"You always was smart," said Masters. "If you can do that, even John Stang'll have to tip his hat."

"It's just damn luck John ain't here." He went into the house and sat behind the desk in the room he used for an office.

He put the injunction on the desk and stared at it. Then he took out a pencil and began figuring on the back of it. He drew a little sketch. He crossed it out and began again. An hour later he sat back and blinked his eyes at the ceiling. It would work, he thought, if every single detail was attended to perfectly by his men.

He could trust them, he had hired them. They were essentially his rather than John Stang's men. Masters was an all-around cattleman and could have worked anywhere except that he had a crooked streak over which he had no control. Jose California with his Mexican costumes and white-toothed grin was not a workman but he had killed a dozen men without ever being arrested or brought to trial. Cooky Harris was even deadlier. As to Dutch Herman—well, he could be eliminated after the event. The hills provided burying places that no one could ever find. No one would discover Beasley —and if such a discovery was made who would ask of the end of that drunken bum?

Yes, it would work. He had to lay it out for them step by step. Dutch Herman would be given the easy part. There wasn't a hole in it now. The advent of the Marshal had been unfortunate to be sure—but it could be made to work for Kay Cross.

He made a tent of the injunction in the fireplace of the ranch house. It took several matches to get it burning because of the stiffness of the paper. He finally poured a cup of coal oil over it. The flames flickered and soon there was only a pile of light ash.

He went out and mounted his horse and got a blanket from the bunkhouse and obliterated all the tracks left by the shootout at the corral. He rode up and down over the smooth dirt so that his horse's hoofs completed the job. Masters and Dutch Herman came in from their burial detail and he sent them for Jose and Cooky. His mind was very clear, he had it all figured out. John Stang would not approve but this was something that had to be done. Maybe it had been somewhat too unlawful before Maylan had come to Kay Cross but now there was no other way out and in fact none half so good, he congratulated himself.

At dark they were gathered at the chosen place. Jose California's dandyism had paid off, each wore a bolero jacket and a wide hat trimmed with tassels about the brim. Tinsley surveyed the terrain once more.

The road came to a narrow place between two bluffs. There were live oaks at its edge, thick with summer foliage. Cooky Harris and Jose were already in the concealment of thick lower branches which extended across the road.

Dutch Herman tended the corpse of Zeke Maylan, which they now placed in heavy brush below the trees. Jake Masters and Tinsley stood together and spoke in low tones.

"I still think we oughta wipe 'em out," said Masters.

"Nothin' I'd like better. But John Stang would smell a rat. To say nothin' of the Valley people."

"What the hell, you said Booker had trouble with Mexes on the way in, him and that nigger. Everybody knows greasers don't never forget a thing like that."

"Pay attention," said Tinsley sharply. "We want the money they got for the cattle. We want to get rid of Maylan's body and let them try and figure out where it come from. That's all we want."

"It could go wrong, Lige. Then what?"

"We laid that trail south, didn't we? If anything goes wrong we drag blankets to the hills, then to the ranch."

"Then what about Dutch?"

"You plant him where you planted Beasley."

"Like maybe they killed each other?"

"Anything people want to think. Nobody'll miss either one of them."

"Dutch could bake a good pie. Give him dried apples and some flour and he sure could bake a good pie."

"I'll bake you a pie myself," said Tinsley angrily. "Just don't argue and make sure this goes right. And no killin'. We'll take care of that later."

"Okay. It'll be a nice little pouch of money."

"You'll get your share," said Tinsley. "That's all you need to think about."

"They're about due if Jose's right. He seen them from 'way up high just before dark."

"Okay. See that you're ready."

"Hell, I'm always ready."

He was when there was a thievery involved, Tinsley knew. There probably were worse hieves than Masters but he had never known one. They would all obey orders, he thought. He had pounded the details into them and they were accustomed to following him. The attack would be unexpected in this quiet country and the odds were a hundred to one that it would all go off as he had planned.

He wondered why he was sweating in the cool of the evening.

It was pitch dark in this spot when he heard them coming down the road from Silver City. He made sure no one was skylined even in this blackness, then took his position beside the thick tree trunk, invisible to those who were approaching. He had no way of knowing the order in which they rode which was a nuisance but not too dangerous. Probably Booker would be in the lead, anxious to get to his partner and Alicia. That stuck in his craw; he had not made any appreciable progress with the girl and he knew Booker also saw her. Now that her father was dead it might make a difference . . . if he played his cards right, if this thing succeeded.

His eyes accustomed to the darkness, he made them out now, coming around a slight bend in the road. There was a man in advance, the others rode close behind him. They were at a slow canter, their horses weary from the long trip. He crouched with every muscle tense. It was all he could do to let them ride past him.

Then he fired his gun and yelled, "Ole," and jumped for the rear rider. He grabbed and struck with his Colt muzzle at the same time. There was a groan and he knew he had struck home. Exultant he dragged the rider from the saddle and threw him beside the road.

Jose and Cooky tumbled from the tree trunk. Each hit a rider. Both of the victims went down hard.

Masters grunted, "Got it. In Booker's saddlebag."

"Check 'em all, it might be a blind."

"I'm checkin'," said Cooky. "These hombres is sure cold-cocked."

Lige turned to where Dutch Herman was carrying the body of the Marshal to the road. He helped arrange it nearby the unconscious victims. The limbs were stiffening but he thought he made it look natural, as if the lawman had ridden in and met his death at the hands of the robbers. He led Maylan's sorrel toward Silver City and turned him loose, knowing the horse would head for the livery stable where he was kept and fed.

Then he made sure of the Razor Edge money by the light of a dark lantern before he led the others in covering track to the hills. In an hour they were back on the old Payson place. He sat down behind his desk and looked at the others.

"Just one more thing," said Masters.

"Cooky and Jose can attend to it. And Dutch."

"Yeah, Dutch. You ride with them."

"What's more to do? We got it, ain't it?" Dutch gestured. "The money, ha?"

"Just a little errand in the hills," said Tinsley. "Won't take long. Then—whiskey for everybody."

"Oh, ja. We celebrate, I guess."

He went out on his last ride dreaming of whiskey and profits. Tinsley breathed a deep sigh and said, "Jake, take what you want of the money. It ain't important. What is important is that Booker's busted flat and we got rid of Maylan's corpse. It was a good night's work."

"Gettin' rid of them two dummies wasn't bad, neither," said Masters. He indicated the money on the desk. "Since there ain't no place to spend it right now, you might stick that in the safe. Take it along on the drive, bust up Silver City for a few days, okay?"

"Okay," said Tinsley. He sat thinking it all over. Now he could admit to himself that he had managed this maneuver because of the girl. If he busted Booker out of the race he would naturally have a better chance. Too bad about her father, but on the other hand that would make her dependent upon another man—and there he was, Lige Tinsley, part owner of Kay Cross, handsome, agreeable and desirous of marrying her, no nonsense or messing around, a real marriage.

John Stang approved of him getting married. Therefore

John could not be against what he had done to further that proposition. When it was all explained, how Dutch had killed the Marshal and because of that Lige had to act, then John would understand.

Still, he thought that he would not go to town and send a telegram to El Paso. Better to let things slide and see what would happen in Quesada after Booker rode in with the dead lawman and his story of being attacked by Mexican bandits and all that. Much better to play foxy right now. He got out a bottle and poured himself a straight shot. His hands shook very little.

It was early daylight when the battered group led by Sam Booker came to Quesada and went directly to Casper's carpenter shop, which was also the funeral establishment of the Valley. They awakened Casper, who came in underwear and hastily donned pants to stare and disbelieve in horror.

Sam said, "We know what happened but we're not talkin' as yet. Put them in the back room, make 'em look nice, please."

"The Marshal and Delaney, why that's terrible. We never had nothin' like this in the Valley."

"Delaney's skull was cracked," said Sam dully. "Just take care of 'em for now."

Ricco said, "I'll give you a hand, Casper." He too had lost the shine of happy youth which he had worn as a mantle all his young years.

Sam walked stiff-legged to the barber shop and awakened Piney Talcott. They sat in the tiny living quarters behind the barber shop and Sam talked.

"That narrow place in the road, you know, with the trees. They come out of the trees, they come out of the brush. We never had a chance. They got all the money, everything."

"But who? Who did it?"

"They wore Mexican hats, yelled 'ole', all that. I waited for daylight to read track. Ricco, he can track as good as anybody, him ridin' the hills a-huntin' all his life. They tried to make us believe it was bandits from below the border, all right. But when you cover track, it's the same as leavin' track unless you're real smart. It was Kay Cross."

"But Zeke? What about Zeke."

"He was dead hours before they hit us. He was stiff as

a board. You go look at Delaney, then look at Zeke. You got that medical trainin' from your father and all. But anybody can see Zeke was dead long before Delaney was killed."

Piney said, "Then they killed Zeke, decided to start the war by stealing our money. They threw in Zeke because it could have been that he rode out to meet you and was caught in the holdup by Mexican bandits."

"You got to figure it that way."

"But the injunction?"

"It wasn't on Zeke. I got your telegram and looked for it. He must have got killed servin' it."

"But the paper itself is not important. We can get another paper from Santa Fe."

"Sure. But first we got to get a new lawman. Then we got to wait until the red tape unwinds. We got no money. And Kay Cross will cut off the water, move in and wipe us out. Paper won't count if we're wiped out."

"But the law. . . ."

"Law in the valley died with Zeke."

Piney said, "Alicia. We've got to tell Alicia."

"Will you go with me?" Sam shook visibly at the prospect of breaking the news.

"Let me get dressed."

Sam sat and waited. The shock and grief were wearing off and the deep revulsion and rage were building. He was a man of his time, he knew answers to the questions. His plan was already half-formulated. He would consult neither Piney nor Alicia in this regard. There were two men, one in Texas and one in or around Lincoln, New Mexico, who had occasion to be obligated to him, who also knew the procedure which was left to him. He would send telegrams as soon as he could get to the Wells Fargo office. He could not fight Kay Cross without aid and these men would bring others of their kind, men with guns who knew how to use them.

It was a grim prospect but he had tried to do it right, to lift himself by his bootstraps and he would have made it, too, with Piney and Alicia and Zeke behind him. Only Kay Cross could have stopped him. Kay Cross had succeeded and it was time to take drastic steps and he was able and willing to do so no matter what the consequences were.

He rubbed the knot on his head. The attack had been masterful, no doubt about it. But the attempts at deception had been pitiful. The only angle in favor of Kay Cross was that there was no court, no law and no real evidence beyond the word of Ricco and himself that the tracks told the true story. It was enough for this time and place he admitted. It was more than enough when the overwhelming strength of Kay Cross, the principals and the riders behind them, already a score or more with the many they could bring into the Valley.

It meant open warfare. It was a terrible situation for the Valley people, the farmers, the townsfolk. They would wish it had never happened and they would not side with Razor Edge, they would be afraid and Sam did not blame them. Nobody wanted to live in the shadow of destruction.

Piney appeared in sober, dark clothing, his hat set squarely on his head, patently suffering. They walked down to the Marshal's office and home. There were very few people awake at this time but she greeted them fully clothed. There was the odor of coffee in the kitchen. She stared at them, her eyes wide.

"It's papa, isn't it?" she said before they could speak. "He never came back from serving the injunction on Kay Cross."

"Yes, it's Zeke." Sam's voice was a croak.

"I knew it." She sat down on a kitchen chair. "He used to think it would come this way. Then here in the Valley it was so quiet he thought it might come with his boots off. I guess I've been prepared for it all my life. I can't even weep."

Sam said, "He's over at Casper's."

"Who did it?" Her voice was low and tremulous but still the tears did not come.

"Somebody at Kay Cross." He told her the story, each painstaking detail.

She said, "Yes. Kay Cross. It has to be."

"They've got our money. They don't even have to cut off the water now. They can but they don't have to."

"Everyone knows about the injunction," she said. "It's all over the valley."

"But no one saw it excepting the Marshal," Piney said. "It'll take time to get another paper to serve and a man to serve it."

"Yes," she said. "They mean to wipe us out."

"They've just about done it. What we got left is culls, a few cows and Clancy. It ain't enough," Sam said.

"Yes. They've got us in a corner."

"We could move on," said Piney. "We could start over and think about it and maybe come back. Razor Edge is ours, we've got a deed to the land."

"We could do that," said Sam. "We could do that or we could just quit. Maybe you'd like to do that."

"What do you mean?" asked Alicia. Her lips trembled but she did not weep.

"We been through it all before." His voice was low and harsh. "Maybe you two could get out, go some place. Me, I got to stay."

Piney said, "He's right, we've been through it before. Maybe Alicia should get out of the Valley until something happens one way or the other. Maybe to Santa Fe, where she could work on her father's connections, try and get some action from the Governor or the legislature."

"But you two will stay?"

"And fight," Sam said. "It was decided long ago."

There was a silence. Then she said, "If you stay—I stay. I think I'd like to go to papa, now."

They did not argue with her. Each in his own way knew that the war was impossible, unequal, but no one now thought of quitting.

CHAPTER SIX

John Stang almost rode two horses to death traveling the hundred miles from El Paso but he missed the funeral. He sat in his room at the hotel in Quesada and listened to Lige Tinsley, his face stony.

"After that dumb bastard killed Maylan, I had to think fast. There was goin' to be hell to pay no matter what. You know Jake, show him a dollar and he'll go along. Then I had to get rid of Dutch because he's a drunk. It wasn't easy to figure this all out and grab Booker's money besides."

"And I didn't want the law broke," said Stang, half to himself. "I thought it would work out."

"There wasn't no way. Not after Beasley and Dutch did what they did."

"You couldn't turn Dutch in?"

"That would've made it look real bad for Kay Cross."

"If you turned him in?"

"No matter. The lawman got hisself killed. The whole Valley is out lookin' for Mexican bandits right now."

"You think Booker's lookin' for 'em, too?"

"I don't give a hoot about Booker now. I got him where I want him."

"Dead and buried?"

"As good as."

"You think that."

Tinsley said, "He's hogtied, no money, no nothin'. And his gal suspects nothin'. She's just the same to me as before."

Stang asked, "How come you didn't burn down Razor Edge and blame that on the greasers?"

"Why burn down good property that'll be Kay Cross's?"

"So Booker is alive and somewhere in the Valley."

"He's got one man, the kid Ricco."

"Uh-huh." Stang sighed. "Well, the fat's in the fire. What you done was dumb but there we are."

"Dumb? I did what had to be done."

"Yeah. Like I say, we're into it. Now you better get the boys and get busy."

"Doin' what? We're sittin' pretty. We make the drive and wait. Booker'll have to get out."

"He will, will he?" Stang pointed a finger at him. "You dumb fool. Beasley and Dutch, they never did have any brains like you're supposed to. You don't know a damn thing about people, you never did, never will. But I'm givin' you an order now. Git out there and find Booker. Kill him and bury him with the others. I don't care how you do it so long as it's done quick."

"You said you didn't want him killed. That the Valley people . . ."

"That was before you lost your damn mind. Now you got to do it. Make it look like the greasers were after him from last year. Anything you want. But kill him. Then we'll buy Razor Edge from the nigger and hope for the best."

"What about the water?"

"You got to cut it off, now. You got to act like you never seen that injunction. If anybody knows you seen it you got a good chance of bein' tried for murder of Zeke Maylan. By God, I thought I'd taught you somethin'. Somewhere along the line I sure missed."

"Now wait a minute, John . . ."

"Furthermore I got a big hunch this is all because of that gal. You couldn't wait. All right, they shot Zeke, you wasn't there. If you'd of cleaned that up. . . . Aggh, never mind. It's done and it's done. Get Booker and get him quick. I'm goin' to Santa Fe on the next stage."

"What about the Eyetalian kid? His old man's the smithy, people like him around here."

"If he's with Booker and the Mexes kill him what of it?"

"Okay, John, if that's the way you want it. It'll be a real pleasure."

"Aw, get outa here. If I ever figured you'd turn out like this. . . . oh, the hell with it."

Tinsley closed the door softly behind him. He went down to the lobby and beckoned Masters outdoors.

"Take Jose and Cooky and get Booker."

"Where do I find him?"

"Start at Razor Edge. But first get them Mex outfits. John liked that notion. Make it look like the greasers."

"Gotcha," said Masters. He hesitated. "John offerin' any reward?"

"A hundred apiece," said Tinsley. It would be worth paying it out of his own pocket, he thought.

"You be along later?"

"Later." He walked down the street. Piney Talcott was shaving a customer. He hesitated, decided to leave the barber for later, when Stang gave further orders. He was smarting all over from the interview in the hotel room.

Main Street was crowded with wagons and pedestrians. Lige spoke to several. He was answered civilly but there was something in the averted glances, the sudden turns to avoid him that gave him pause. He had been vociferous in his threats against the invading Mexicans, no one had disputed him. There seemed no reason why they should now have turned against him.

He stopped at the Marshal's home, tapped on the side door. Alicia, wearing a plain black dress, opened and allowed him to enter. He sat in the parlor, hat on his knees.

"If you need anything, Lishia?"

"Father provided for me. He was a lawman, you know. He knew his life was often in danger."

"Yes. Well, what can I say? You know how I feel about you. I'll wait until you feel better for sure. But you know."

"Thank you," she said. "It'll be a long while before I can —be myself. In any way."

"Sure, that's right. It's too bad about Sam, losin' his stake and all."

"We all lost a lot," she told him. "It was a great tragedy for the Valley and everyone in it."

"That's for sure."

"Excepting Kay Cross, of course."

"Why, Lishia, me and John, we thought the world of Zeke. He was an old friend of John's."

"Yes. I'd forgotten."

"I'll stop by whenever I'm in town," he promised.

"That'll be very nice of you." She managed a weak smile.

He took his leave. On Main Street he encountered Tom Mason.

"It was a nice service," he said. "I suppose you're thinkin' of a new Marshal?"

"No. We haven't anyone to take Zeke's place."

"Well, it's a quiet town. And Kay Cross will be lookin' for those greasers."

"Will you be working with Sam?"

"Sure will. You happen to know where he is right now?"

"He rode out," said Mason vaguely. "He was feeling pretty bad. Maybe he's going to try and trail the bandits."

"Could be. Well, I'll be seein' you." He untied his horse and rode out toward Kay Cross.

In the kitchen of the house on Razor Edge Ricco talked with Sam Booker. "I put Clancy and the cows in the arroyo. You know? The one they'll never find. There's a cave, too. I put three guns and all the shells I could find in there. I was sorry to miss the funeral. My father understands, he gave me one of the guns, a Sharps, it carries a lot further than ordinary rifles. Right?"

"You did well," said Sam. He was cleaning the last of four rifles. A shotgun leaned ready in a corner. His Colt was newly oiled and a twin hung in a spare gunbelt on a peg. A thirteen-inch Bowie was on the table. "I found the dynamite and the detonators and some wire. We may need it."

Ricco said, "There's a leak of water in the back of the cave. There are blankets and mama sent plenty food, dry and for cookin' if we dare make a fire."

"Not 'we' Ricco. Me."

"You don't know these hills as I do," said the young man, showing his remarkably white teeth. "You'd be lost without me. Lishia knows the hills better than you." He sobered. "And this is my fight. The fight for the Valley, my place. Papa agrees, mama agrees. We talked about it."

Sam said, "It's my fight. I don't want to drag anybody into it."

Ricco tapped the lump on his head. "They slugged me, too. On every score it's my fight as well as it's yours. And you need me, Sam, you need me in the hills."

"I don't like it."

"And they killed my pardner," said Ricco softly. "That old man, that Jack Delaney, he taught me plenty about cattle. He was a wise old man. When they killed him they brought vendetta from this Italian."

"Vendetta? What's that?"

"It's what you people call a feud. Only with Italians it is quicker and hotter, no waitin' generations to kill the enemy. Wherever and whenever—we kill."

"That's a feud in Tennessee," said Sam. "Reckon I can't argue against you."

"I think we'd better get goin'," said Ricco. "I think Kay Cross will be looking for us."

"What else can they do? I want them to look for us."

"Yes. Me, too, I want them looking."

They gathered the weapons and boxes of cartridges. Sam took a last look around the house. He had dwelt in it for a year and Alicia had fixed it up a lot. He had thought it might be his home forever. He hunched his shoulders and carried the weapons outside and packed them on a horse. There were two pack horses and the best of the Razor Edge string, a bay he liked to ride and a swift black for Ricco.

They rode up the winding trail of the mesa behind the house. Ricco was aiming for shale beyond, where their tracks would be impossible to follow. Sam looked back once, then said, "Hold up."

"Ah, yes, they are coming for us already." Ricco rode

around a bend behind heavy cholla and some pinons. They dismounted and tied up. Then they crept back across the mesa, rifles in their hands, watching the Kay Cross men come in from below.

There were Masters and Jose and Cooky Harris and a half-dozen riders who had abandoned the roundup for the funeral at Tinsley's orders. They rode into the yard and hallooed.

Ricco whispered, "It's a nice chance to pick 'em off."

"Too many of them," said Sam.

"We could chance it, maybe?"

"I just couldn't," Sam admitted. "The time may come but it's against my habits."

"Vendetta," said Ricco.

"You're right. But I can't do it now."

They had learned that no one was at home. They dismounted, examined the empty corral. Ricco had turned out all the horses to pasture. They looked in the barn and one of them called to Masters.

"Hey, Jake. The bull ain't nowheres around."

Masters stomped to the corral, looked for track. "Looks like they lit a shuck. Jose, you make anything out of it?"

The dapper California shrugged. "They go. The hills, Ricco knows the hills, people say."

"Then we'll have to comb them out."

"Better have big comb. They got high gun, better have plenty men. An army?"

"Better see Lige. Better see what he says."

"He wants the bull, that's a fine seed bull."

"He ain't gonna get him right off," said Cooky Harris. "Two men, knowin' them hills, they can raise hell."

On the plain of the mesa Ricco said to Sam, "They don't know nothin' yet. Why don't we pick off a couple of 'em right now? You heard them. Sooner or later, why not now?"

"We got packs," said Sam. He was boiling but the odds were too great. "Better to wait."

"They killed Jack."

"I know. They'll do worse before they're through, maybe. But best we wait."

They watched the Kay Cross bunch leave without doing damage. They mounted and rode into the hills. Ricco led the way over terrain he had hunted since he was a small boy. They came to the arroyo concealed by thick brush at the south entrance and began the two-man siege against the powerful, ruthless Kay Cross outfit.

It was the life of outlaws, Sam Booker thought. They were marked men, they could not move in daylight. They would live by night. He had hope of help. But as of now he was lonely for Alicia, for Piney, for the life he had hoped to lead in the Valley of Quesada.

Ricco, on the other hand, was ebullient, happy to be in the hills. He loved the country, he loved the rigors of camping in the cave. To him it was pure adventure. He had brought black clothing to wear at night on the black horse.

"They'll never see me, much less catch me," he told Sam. "Free as the air. I'll ride through and around them and among them. We can go to town any night. We got Piney and we got Alicia and Tom Mason."

"And a damp cave to live in. And two dozen gunnies lookin' to shoot us on sight."

"They will never sight us before we get a bead on them," said Ricco.

"They can bring in a hundred more men. You don't know how big they are."

"I don't care," said Ricco from the inexperience of his youth. "I welcome them. They want war, we will give them war."

"That's my intention, to give 'em war," said Sam. "But I don't have to like it."

He chewed on a biscuit, washed it down with cold water. He knew too well the cost of war against an outfit like Kay Cross.

Ricco said, "I think we'll ride tonight. They won't expect us, huh?"

"Yeah. We'll ride tonight." He needed action, he could not squat in a cave with his girl in town and his ranch deserted and all the money gone and the odds so great. Whatever could be done he wanted it done quickly. He felt better thinking that they would ride at night.

Piney was asleep when the soft knock came at his door. He arose and donned trousers and a shirt without lighting the lamp. A tall, thin man spoke in a whisper.

"Talcott? I'm Benson."

"Come in."

The shades were tightly drawn. The lamp shone on a face

lined with years of outdoor living, sharp dark eyes, a thin mouth turned down at the corners.

Piney asked, "You're Shag Benson?"

The man produced a telegraph signed by Sam Booker. "I'm him. From up no'th. Damme if you ain't a nigra."

"I'm Sam's partner."

"Damme. I was in Jefferson with a nigra years back. Best damn man I ever knew. They beat him to death but they nevah made him quit. Name o' Johnson. Big buck, full of nerve."

"We like to think color doesn't measure a man."

Benson said, "That's what I learned. He learned me, Johnson did. Jail couldn't put him down. He died brave."

Piney said, "You know what's going on, I take it."

"I know Kay Cross. And I know Sam. He bit off a big chaw, from what I hear along the way."

"He's in the hills."

"How do I find him?"

Piney hesitated, then said reluctantly, "I'll have to get Alicia Maylan. She's the only one can take you there."

"Zeke's gal, huh? Heard about Zeke, too. Did Kay Cross get him?"

"We can't prove it. But they got him."

Benson said, "He got me one time. Threw down on me afore I could move a finger. Must've been a crossfire to blast Zeke."

"That's what we believe."

"He was a good man."

"Yes. He was a fine man."

"Hadn't I better move out afore somebody sees me?"

"I'll go for Alicia."

He walked the back way to the dwelling behind the jail. She came to the door at his low call.

"Benson?"

"Yes."

She said, "He's an outlaw, you know. But a decent man. Go back and tell him I'll be there as soon as I get dressed."

"I don't like this, Lishia," he said. "You riding out at night with an outlaw and all Kay Cross looking for Sam."

"Think of papa," she said simply. "Think of Delaney."

"I'm thinking of them and of you and Sam and Ricco."

"I know. War is always bad."

"You're right." He went to the door. "I'll get the horses."

"Horses?"

"If it's a war I'm enlisted." He hustled away before she could object. He had learned to ride during the year of happiness and good fortune. He was slightly afraid to trust a horse in the dark but he knew he could not sit in his room and chew his nails until Alicia's safe return.

The horses were kept at Camponetta's smithy for the sake of secrecy. They were dark chestnuts for night riding. The burly blacksmith helped saddle them.

"My boy, he says do not worry, he's gonna be all right. I do not believe this," he said. "But I believe what he is doing. Go with God."

Walking the horses to the rear of the barber shop was a weird and lonely experience. The town was asleep, there was no one stirring, even Finnegan's was closed. Piney wondered how many of the inhabitants would inform upon them if the occasion arose. A few, he thought, but very few. Tom Mason had stirred most of Quesada into smouldering rage, a helpless rage in the face of Kay Cross strength.

Benson and Alicia were waiting. She wore men's clothing, which Piney had provided; they were about the same size if not of the same dimensions. They huddled in the darkness.

Benson said, "This is kinda hairbrained, ain't it, ma'am? I mean, this is a poor pitiful bunch to go agin Kay Cross."

"It is."

He nodded. "Meanin' if I don't cotton to it I should pull out now. Well, ma'am, it ain't what you call a lead pipe cinch any of us'll live to tell about it. But meantime I believe we can make it one hiyu war. People like us, we ain't got much more to lose—but we got a lot to gain."

They rode out to the hills. Alicia led them over the shale, down the rough trail and to the entry of the arroyo. When they came to the cave Sam and Ricco were saddled and ready to ride.

"Lishia, what are you doing . . ." Sam spotted Benson. "Well, Shag you made it. You alone?"

"For now. Got some people comin'." He jerked a thumb at his companions. "You got good help right here."

"The best," said Sam. "Ricco, this here is Shag Benson, a cattleman."

"Then can we hit that south pasture herd tonight?"

Sam said, "How many head could you hold 'til your people get here, Shag?"

"Accordin' to where I get to hold 'em."

"There's a canyon. Ricco and me could help a bit. What we need is men to drive 'em to the border, swim 'em over at night and sell 'em."

Benson said slowly, "So that's the scheme. They'll be on your trail, you know that."

"That's why we need the men."

Benson said, "If it was anybody but Kay Cross it wouldn't work. As it is, I got my doubts. Howsome ever, my men will fight if they get a big enough share."

"I don't figure on takin' the money," said Sam. "I figure on gettin' mine back another way."

"They owe you, do they?"

"They owe me two lives and the sale of our herd," said Sam. "They owe me a time and a place I had for the three of us, and for Ricco, too, because Ricco is part of us. You got any more questions, Shag?"

"Why, no. The way you tell it, I got to believe."

"You'll be in charge of your people. Ricco and me, we'll pick the spots."

Benson said, "I'm beginnin' to kinda like it, at that."

"Lishia, you and Piney better go back to town now," Sam said. "It's time to ride."

"No," said Alicia. "If they pick up track and see two, three extra horses they'll wonder. And worry."

"But they might have some people out there, shootin' back."

"There was shooting when papa died." She had contained her grief amazingly well, now the passion in her voice was unmistakable, implacable. "I ride with you."

Piney said, "She's right. Maybe we won't be much help but we carried our rifles."

"It ain't reasonable," Sam said, knowing he was defeated. "It's no place for a gal."

"It's a place for papa's daughter," she told him.

The night was dark but clear. Ricco and Alicia knew every foot of the ground they traveled. The herd they wanted was the farthest from the home ranch of Kay Cross. It was a small bunch but it was prime beef, quickly salable even after losing a few pounds on a fast trek to the border a hundred miles or less away.

The cattle was drowsing in grama grass to its bellies. A rider hunched in the saddle rode slowly at its edges. The roundup had been interrupted by events which did not concern him, he was earning his small pay without interest, Piney thought. Small animals whisked through the buffalo grass, lizards awoke and slithered from beneath the hooves of their horses as they paused on a sloping hillside.

Sam said, "There'll be another hand in his blankets. We don't want to shoot these people if we can help it."

Benson said, "I'll make a pasear. Young fella, can you play Injun real good?"

"Since I was a boy," said Ricco.

They dismounted and moved in opposite directions, unbuckling their spurs as they went like shadows into deeper shadows. The others waited, holding the noses of their mounts, speaking in whispers. Piney felt suddenly lost as in a dream, a wild nightmare of a dream. How had he come here, to this hill on a deep night to steal cattle? He was a barber from New York City, yet he had a rifle in a scabbard and beside him was a beautiful woman dressed as a man and beyond her was a Tennesseean raised in Texas and toughened by the vagaries of frontier life and it was not at all like the stories in the magazines which he had avidly read in his father's shop.

"Benson is the best scout I ever knew," Sam was whispering. He was nervous, on edge because of Alicia's presence. "Ricco and him, they'll take care of those two. Now you stay up here with your rifles in case you're needed, hear me? Don't come down there, us three can drive the critters to the canyon."

"I know the canyon," said Alicia. "I know as much of the hills as Ricco."

"What good can you do? I tell you the three of us can do it and you should get back to town."

"What about the riders down there?"

"They'll be tied up. They'll never know what hit 'em."

"It sounds good," said Alicia. "If nothing goes wrong."

"Nothin's goin' wrong," said Sam. "We're goin' to hit them and hit them again until they bleed. Sooner or later we're goin' to get at Tinsley and the gunnies. Sooner or later. You mark my words."

Piney believed him. He spoke in a guttural, the black rage shimmering through his words which were more threat than oration, spoken in a way Sam had not used before.

Pure hatred lay beneath the speech and Piney shivered despite himself.

Then he detected that all the time Sam was talking he was holding Alicia's hand. The act imbued him with the feeling that this was indeed a holy crusade—a fight against evil. He self-consciously looked away from the loving couple, toward the top of the hill. A flicker of moonlight peered through the clouds.

He saw a rider, then another, then two more coming down the hill toward them. He stabbed Sam with a forefinger even as he reached for the gun in the boot attached to his saddle.

Sam said, "Damn, they're comin' to move this herd in." He pulled his six-shooter and fired twice in the air to warn Benson and Ricco, holding the reins of their horses, speaking savagely to Alicia and Piney, "You ride in, you got to!"

The Kay Cross men lost no time, stood upon no ceremony. Piney, who felt the wind of bullets seeking the flash of Sam's Colt, yanked Alicia to earth. The horses plunged—and then out of the night arose Benson, who helped with the ponies, drawing his revolver, shooting at the men charging down the hill. It was, Piney thought with shock, a cavalry versus an infantry engagement; there was dire danger here, the worst he had ever dreamed of encountering.

He fired his rifle and his aim was good enough to send a horse floundering and screaming to the night. Alicia held her father's sixgun in both hands, shooting at the vague forms of those who represented to her no more than the murderers of the Marshal, Piney knew. She had no thought of running away and it steadied him and he touched the trigger again and a man pitched sideways and was dragged wildly down the hill.

Ricco came sliding into join them and said breathlessly, "Got the sleepin' one."

Benson drawled, "That makes two. But this is another matter. They got fire power there."

The charge had been broken. The Kay Cross riders were scattering. Sam fired twice at moving targets and missed. Alicia was reloading the revolver beside Piney on the ground. There was no cover, he realized, it would be a pitched battle, the odds about even.

Sam clamped his arm in a grip which hurt. "Take her in, Piney. Take her in!"

"We don't want to leave you here," she said.

"You go in. It ain't worth a damn if you don't. You listen to me, you go in."

Piney said, "He's right. We might get in the way. We don't know how to fight this kind of fight."

She said, "No," but Piney took her arm. Leading the horses he pulled her down the hill. She was reluctant but she finally saw the reason for going. They went past the herd and to the road. The firing continued on the hillside.

"He'll be killed," she said, weeping now as she had not for her dead father. "I can't lose them both, Piney, I can't."

He said, "He gave us orders. It's best to follow orders when you're not sure."

He got her on the horse and they rode toward town. The moon vanished and it was pitch black. The horses knew the road. Piney's heart pounded with the sound of the hooves. The girl wept as she rode.

When Alicia and Piney were out of sight it was as though a giant hand had been lifted from Sam Booker. There was sporadic firing from the Kay Cross men. They had taken positions with no belly for another charge. He reloaded his rifle and his mind began to work again, as it could not when the girl was in danger.

"Shag."

"Right here. Reckon we better skedaddle?"

"Yeah." He was able to chuckle. "Right at the herd."

Ricco said, "They're fat and lazy. Maybe they won't stampede."

"Then we get through."

"We could get caught among 'em," said Benson. "I seen it happen. Have to use muzzle fire, shoot our way."

"Steal 'em or kill 'em just so Kay Cross don't have 'em," said Sam. "I ain't for runnin' from Kay Cross."

"You got to, sooner or later."

"Sure. But not without harmin' them."

Ricco said, "I'm with Sam."

"It ain't sensible." Benson sighed. "Howsome ever, man's only got one life and I'm beginnin' to take a pure dislike to them rannies with guns out there. One of 'em put a hole in my hat."

"Listen." A man was moaning for help which did not

come. "We put some holes where it did some good. Let's spread out a bit and come in from below."

They walked the horses in the night, each step one that could well be the last. There were bullets flying but not too close, Sam thought. The Kay Cross men were fighting in the dark, disorganized. The leaders were not out tonight, these were cowhands, tough enough but ignorant gunslingers, the kind that made neither great cattlemen nor great killers.

The herd, sluggish from the long grazing or not, was milling, skittish from unaccustomed night sound and action. There were no herders to sing them to their nightly soporific contentment. When the three riders suddenly came at them sixguns blazing, they wheeled and began lumbering from danger. Sam and his companions whooped and hollered and swung coiled lariats against their withers as they ran.

Now the Kay Cross men began firing at the herd, trying to pick out a rider, a target. It became uncomfortably hot. There was no prospect of stealing the cattle that night, Sam knew, they would be followed too closely. He made himself shoot down a steer, a deed he hated but which he knew must be accomplished. Frightened, running cattle rumbled over the corpse, piled up.

Benson shouted, "Better cut out now."

"Follow Ricco," Sam called back. "He knows the way."

Ricco pulled off as the stampede went westward. Benson fell in behind him. Sam pulled into the rear and twisted in the saddle, resuming the rifle for this maneuver. He caught a Kay Cross man aiming at him and shot the man down. He thought of Zeke now, and of Jack Delaney dead of a broken skull. He fired several times, not knowing whether or not he scored, his anger directing the gun muzzle. Then they were riding in Ricco's wake to the ever-changing, rolling, dipping, rising, tangling hills toward the arroyo and the cavern.

When they had tended the horses they were voraciously hungry. They opened tins, wary of making a fire lest pursuers might stumble on their retreat.

Benson said, "Never saw it to fail. Fight and eat."

"It was hard luck," Sam grieved. "Nothin' gained but some blood. To hurt them you got to take cattle. They can hire new hands, they got the money."

"The boys'll be here," Benson told him. "I seen enough tonight to know there'll be profits."

"We got to take small bunches," Sam said. "The best they breed but small bunches."

"They won't follow my boys," said Benson. "Not unless they want to be buried where they lay."

"You sure we can handle them boys?"

"They got the same choice. Take orders or be buried."

It was true, Sam reflected. Shag Benson was a hard one. He had rustled cattle up and down the land for years. He had killed his share of men and in him was a lack of caring, an indifference to life or death which was chilling at times. Yet he was a pleasant man, he smiled a lot. He was known to be as good as his word, better than many a respectable citizen. In a fight like this the only question was how far did a man go to regain his own.

It was a decision he had already made, he realized. He would not have reckoned cost except for Alicia. When he thought of her his heart swelled and his mind fogged over in spots. A man in love, he thought, was never again a whole man, something had been given to the woman, effecting a change in him which could never be repaired. He chewed upon a bit of jerky, quelling an uneasiness, a trepidation which was not fear for himself.

Piney and Alicia huddled behind the Marshal's office and jail cells under a tree that shaded the dwelling quarters. She was in control of herself but she was, he realized, shaken.

"What if they killed him?" she asked for the tenth time. "What will we do?"

"They won't kill Sam." He was not at all certain but he had to console her as best he could.

She said, "Tomorrow, I'm moving out, you know."

"I didn't know."

She sighed. "So, so much excitement. This house is town property, but we own a little house on Wayne Street, near the Camponetta's place. Mr. and Mrs. Camponetta are moving me. I'll be glad."

"But you made such a nice home here."

"For papa. I don't know, Piney, I'm all mixed up. If it wasn't for you I think I'd go crazy."

He gulped. No one, much less a white woman had ever addressed him in those exact terms. It put an enormous responsibility upon him.

"Whatever I can do," he said. "Sam will be slipping into

town whenever he can. Maybe when John Stang comes back we can arrange something."

"It's too late. Far too late. They drew blood, Piney. You must understand, they killed. It's a war we saw out there tonight." She was impressively intent on making him fully understand.

"I can't get it into my head," he murmured. "I shot a man tonight. I don't know, helping Sam when he was attacked by the bandits was different. Maybe I'm not up to it, Alicia."

"You stood up to Lige. That wasn't easy."

"But I saw what happened there, too. How he didn't care if he ran down Tommy Mason. If you see it happen, you can fight the injustice. I guess I'm truly different from other folks."

She said very seriously, "Piney I don't want to hear such talk. We think as much of you as if you were our brother, Sam and me."

"I'm a black man. This country is the best I've seen, it gives me a chance. But truthfully I don't know if I'm up to it."

"Be yourself," she advised. "You'll find your place."

"Even if it's the graveyard. They tell me down South a Negro can't be buried in a white folks graveyard. Here—it can be Boot Hill."

"Don't talk like that, either," she said. "We'd better go and get some sleep. We'll have news tomorrow. Sam wouldn't let us be without news."

"Good night, Alicia."

"Goodnight, Piney, my friend."

He was her friend and Sam's partner but he had to sneak through back ways in the dark and not only because of the need for secrecy for what had happened that night. There were some people who would have been aghast at the fact of his close association with Alicia, with his meeting alone with her. He trailed his rifle into the rear door of the shop and sank exhausted onto his bed.

Alicia may be right, he thought, but how can she know, or how can Sam know what it's like to be black? He was the first generation out of the deep south, out of slavery. His father had been a freedman but had never lost his slave philosophy. His father had been right out of "Uncle Tom's Cabin," a bad book that had such a terrific influence. The place that he, Piney, had tried to make in New Mexico was a special place and one fraught with deep dangers even without a range war. Even Alicia, whom he loved, could not know the deep depths here involved.

Wearily he arose, picked up the rifle, cleaned it, oiled it and reloaded it. He replaced it in the corner of the shop where it stood unobtrusively each day. If they ever found out he had been on the raid of Kay Cross cattle he would be automatically dead and he knew it well. His anguish lay in the fact that he was neither prepared to die nor did he know how well he could die.

Lige Tinsley hooked a knee over the pommel of his Texas saddle and listened to the man named Cobey, whose arm was in a sling, whose eyes were red from lack of sleep and whose lip trembled whenever he stopped speaking. The dead animals were already being picked over by vultures. Gnawed at the previous night by coyotes, they were not even worth anything for beef. There was a grave on the hillside where they had buried Alfredo, the dead cowboy.

Tinsley asked, "How many would you guess there was of 'em?"

"They kept movin'," said Cobey. "Seemed like there was a passel of 'em."

"You couldn't count?"

"I was better able than the other boys 'cause I was down early and I couldn't count. It was pitch black."

Jake Masters said, "Booker, the ginney kid Ricco. You reckon the nigger was out there?"

"Niggers don't fight gun battles," said Lige. "I don't figure on the nigger."

"There was more'n two of 'em," declared Cobey. "Hell's bells, the shot was flyin' like bees around my ears."

"Take two men, they know the lay of the land, they move and shoot fast, it could be," said Masters. "How the hell could Booker get more men here so soon? I figure at least the nigger."

"No nigger'd have the sand," Tinsley said. "You think he don't know what we'd do to him? You think he wants to get flayed and have his black skin hung on the barn door?"

Cooky Harris drawled, "You forget, Lige, this here's a Yankee nigger. Yankee niggers don't know."

"Uppity, book-readin' nigger," said Masters. Jose California came riding in to the group. He shook his head. "The stampede, too much. But more than two, si. Maybe three. Maybe more."

"If it's any other damn man in the Valley we'll cut him down along with Booker," vowed Masters.

"First we catch 'em, no?" California showed his teeth. "We ride?"

"We ride," said Tinsley. But when he looked at the ranging hills he knew it was a long chance. White clouds nestled around the mountain tops which were everywhere on the rim of the high plain. It was a perfect day but he didn't see it, he was thirsting for the blood of Sam Booker. As they wheeled toward the hills he drew his revolver and shot four times at the buzzards, hitting two of them, not disturbing the others at their grisly feast.

"Prime beef," he grunted. "The bastards killin' prime beef. I catch that Booker alive, he'll hang for this."

He rode past the grave of the dead cowboy Alfredo without glancing at the fresh mound of earth. Kay Cross paid top wages, forty a month and found with bonuses if there was shooting and those who were hired took their chances, he figured.

But the extra rider or riders with Booker, that was something to figure out. He hadn't thought of outside help; he had believed they would easily deal with Sam and Ricco, picking them off sooner or later. Now the roundup was hampered by this new development, furthermore it would be risky to hit the trail for Silver City with snipers riding the fringe, hiding in the hills, taking their shots as they called them, dropping men and cattle.

Booker had moved fast, too fast, much faster than Tinsley had imagined. It was smart and he hadn't thought Sam was smart. Gun-quick, a good cowman, a fighter, but dumb, he had thought.

Masters reined in beside him, his face bright with an idea. "Lige. How about Injuns?"

"Apaches? They been on the reservations. They ain't out this year."

"Always some young bucks out. Always. Maybe Booker or the Ricco kid know some loco braves. Maybe they want beef."

"Did you look at them dead cows?"

"Yeah. I looked."

"You see any beef cut?"

"Well, no. But there was shootin' and it was dark."

"Hungry Apaches would've cut beef."

Masters was dejected. "If it ain't the nigger and it ain't Injuns then I'm stumped."

"We'll learn who it is."

"I swan to ginney when I do it'll go harder for 'em, makin' me sweat them out like this."

They rode on into the hills. They rode up and down. They lost track almost immediately on rock outcropping, slid on slippery shale. The sun shone unmercifully upon them and they could not seem to find water this far west and south of the ranch countryside. At noon Tinsley knew it was hopeless. Even Jose California was at a loss.

He said, "All right. Get that south pasture herd together. Pull it closer to the house. Jake, Jose, Cooky, you come with me."

"You makin' me a straw boss?" asked Cobey. "I got to get some sleep."

"Pick out some men to do the job. You're captain when Jake ain't around, you know the men. You got an extra twenty for the arm. Lucky it wasn't the bone."

"I can manage the arm, and thank'ee." Cobey held his shoulders a little straighter as he rode for the middle ranch, where there were more Kay Cross men at work.

Masters said, "He's okay, Lige. You picked a good 'un."

"He took a bullet, he'll want to fight back," said Tinsley. "I want haters after Booker."

He left them at the old Payson place, changing clothes, saddling up a fresh mount, riding to Quesada. He went into the barber shop. Piney was shaving Tom Mason. Tinsley took a seat, stretched out his legs, surveying the handmade boots with red stitching.

"Had a fracas on the south pasture last night. You seen your pardner, Mister Talcott?"

"No, Mister Tinsley," said Piney.

"A fight? Anybody hurt?" asked Mason.

"One dead, one hurt. You happen to know where your pardner Booker is at, Mister Talcott?"

Piney finished with the razor and brought the chair up to sitting position as he wiped Mason's face with a tepid towel. From the rear of the shop the burly figure of Camponetta strolled to a seat next to Tinsley. The smithy nodded without speaking, his face unreadable.

Casper, the husky carpenter-undertaker came in the front door wearing his apron upon which clung shavings. The townsmen all were silent, looking into the mirror, where Tinsley could see the reflection of their grave expressions.

Piney said, "If Sam's not at the ranch he may be anywhere. He's not feeling so good these days."

"And Ricco?" Tinsley turned to the blacksmith, at the same time loosening his revolver holster, sensing danger like a cornered wolf. "Ricco is with Sam, I expect."

"Ricco also does not feel so good," said Camponetta. "Lots people don't feel so good."

"Well, losin' a man and some prime beef, I don't feel so good neither." He got up with care, keeping them all in his range of vision. They were not fighters of course but in their implacable regard he felt danger. "Looks like there might be trouble hereabouts. Too bad, Kay Cross didn't want trouble."

"I'm real sorry for Kay Cross," said Casper. "Sorrier for Alicia Maylan, though."

Tinsley said, "Reckon we're all sorry about that. Good day, gentlemen. And Mister Talcott."

"Good day, Mister Tinsley," said Piney without emotion.

On the street people bowed or acknowledged his presence but without a smile or a gesture of good will. He walked down to the telegraph office and sent a cryptic wire to John Stang in Santa Fe, a code message that spelled trouble in the Valley. Then he strode back to the Marshal's headquarters. It was empty. The house was empty.

He was about to leave, completely at a loss, when Alicia came around the corner of the building carrying a bridle. He stared at her.

"You moved out?"

"Oh, Lige . . . Yes, it's town property."

"Have they appointed a Marshal?"

"Not yet."

"Maybe I'll apply for the job."

"It's elective, you know." She walked toward the house on Wayne Street and he fell in step with her.

"Alicia, we got raided last night. Man killed, another hurt. I know it was Sam."

"Oh? You saw Sam?"

Now people were greeting Alicia warmly, offering help, smiling but not looking at Tinsley. It was a strange sensation, as though he were not really there, not walking with her. As though he did not exist in the minds of Quesada people. His anger grew but he concealed it as best he could.

They came to the modest house and she stopped and he knew he could not enter because she now lived alone and could deny him with impunity.

He asked again, "Do you know where Sam is?"

"Then you didn't see him."

"I'd like to talk to him. There's going to be big trouble if Sam and me don't palaver."

"There's already big trouble. Why don't you find out who killed my father and Jack Delaney and bring them in? You can do it, Lige." She spoke gravely and without animosity.

"I'm trying. For your sake. You ought to know that."

"I like to believe it. You've been nice to me."

"I want to be nicer." He was encouraged by her grave acceptance, as if the status remained quo. "I want to do a lot for you, Alicia. When you feel better, when all this is over I want to talk with you about that."

"When that time comes."

"But I can see you. We might ride out together."

"And be shot at? Oh, no. We might meet here in town, where people can see us. You understand—my reputation."

"These people—they stare at me. Like I'm guilty of somethin'."

"When their Marshal was killed they became nervous, worried. It's always been peaceful in the Valley."

"My men went all the way to the border," he lied. "No sight of any bandits, any gang of riders."

"But you're still trying."

He improvised. "Two of our men are still on the trail, Beasley and Dutch Herman. They'll stick until they find out somethin'."

"That's fine, Lige. I do appreciate it."

"Will you tell Sam I want to see him?"

"If I see him."

"John will be back and we got to talk things over. You know we don't want trouble in the Valley."

"Oh, yes I'm sure you don't." She smiled wanly at him.

He took her hand. "I know you feel bad. You get Sam to palaver, and everything'll turn out all right."

"I'll do my best."

"Angels can do no more." He gave her his best women-killer smile. "And you're an angel."

He left her to think that over, not noticing that the smile had tightened, nor how she stared after him.

CHAPTER SEVEN

Three men rode in at night and were introduced to Sam and Ricco. They had no patronyms, it seemed, they were Kid, Wooden and Cactus. They had hard, mahogany faces and they spoke little and smiled less. They were polite but somewhat inhuman, they listened very carefully to Shag Benson, nodding from time to time, paying little attention to Sam or Ricco.

They rode down to the southern pasture on another moonless night. They killed the two Kay Cross herders and started a hundred or so head of cattle for the border. Benson went with them. Sam and Ricco returned to the cave in the hills. Ricco said, "They are badmen, Sam. Real badmen."

"And good at their job."

"Very good. Sam, I found something today, didn't have time to tell you before."

"Yeah?"

"I was scouting, you know. I rode through one of the blind canyons, looking for a spot to maybe hold some cattle. I found two graves."

"Fresh ones?"

"Fresh enough. I took a look. It's Beasley and Dutch Herman. Shot to death."

"Those two, eh? That settles it."

"You figure it like I do?"

"Zeke got in a crossfire, killed one or both of them, was himself killed. What else?"

"Then they dumped him on us."

"We knew that already."

"It had to be Jake Masters and his boys."

"It wasn't Santa Claus and his elves." Sam cocked an ear, picked up his rifle. "Visitors."

They took positions outside the cavern, behind rocks large enough to conceal them. Then they recognized Alicia and Piney toiling up the steep grade. Sam's heart flipped over, his grin spread to his ears. When she stepped down from the horse into his arms the world changed into a different place, roseate with dreams. He did not even know that Ricco and Piney had taken care of the ponies, leaving them alone. He only knew that everything he cared about was close to him for that moment.

After a minute they went deep inside the cave and lay upon the blankets. She was sweet and demanding. They made love simply, wanting each other, reckless of all else.

Then he lit a cigaret of his making and they talked. He told her of the raid and she nodded gravely, knowing what must be done. He told her of Ricco's discovery and his theory and her eyes flashed when she recognized that her father had died fighting and then she wept a little, but there were not many tears in her, the hatred and desire for vengeance were too strong for tears.

She said, "We brought as much tinned goods as we could and Ricco's mama baked Italian cakes for him."

"That's fine, we get tired of Kay Cross beef."

"Stang is in town. He and Lige still tell everyone they want to talk with you, settle everything peaceably. And everybody knows they want to get you in a corner and kill you."

"The town knows?"

"Tom Mason helps. We keep the town informed. The farmers are not fighters, you know. Neither are the townsfolk but they'll stay silent and they don't believe Kay Cross lies."

"I worry about you and Piney, sittin' ducks for 'em if they come into the open."

"Don't fret. The town watches over us."

"Yeah, but Kay Cross has brought in more men, they got an army now. Once or twice they almost stumbled on this place. If they do, there'll be a whale of a fight."

"You've got high gun," she said, refusing to worry. "I almost wish it would come to that if only I could be here."

He shook his head. "It ain't what we planned, is it? A nice house, cattle runnin' the graze, a quiet life, you and me and Piney on Razor Edge. It didn't work out."

"It will, darling, it will." She was indomitable. "They can't come to the Valley and destroy it. They can't."

"They're tryin' real hard." Sometimes it seemed hopeless.

"The good Lord won't let them."

They went to the mouth of the cave. Piney and Ricco were watching, rifles cradled. Ricco motioned toward the plain far below.

"Party just went out. They'll be chasin' Benson."

"They won't like it when they catch him."

"I bet they won't. Shag'll be ridin' drag just in case. I swear that man's the fastest shot I ever did see."

"He never misses, either. He'd be a dead man if he did. Shag's been in so many cattle wars he don't know how to behave out of one." He said to Piney, "You're real quiet tonight. Anything botherin' you special, pardner?"

"Just about everything," Piney said frankly. "I reckon I'm scared."

"Just keep cuttin' hair and razorin' beards," Sam said. "It'll work out. We still own Razor Edge."

"It's deserted. It sickens me to see it deserted."

"It makes us all sick," said Alicia. "We better be getting back home. We have to be up early in case they're watching."

She kissed Sam long and hard. Ricco brought the horses and they started the ride through the back trails she knew so well. They were silent for a long time, then Alicia spoke.

"You think I'm hard, vengeful, unwomanly, don't you, Piney?"

"No," he said quickly. "But I still wish you and Sam would get married, go away, let me sell out. We could start over again, my trade would keep us until we found our place. I'm scared. I'm scared of losing you and Sam. I'm scared of our very lives. We almost had it made and now—blood and death all around us. I have nightmares."

"Poor Piney," she said. "Yes, I have nightmares. It is a hard time for us."

"They'll bring in more gunslingers. They can raise an army. I think they're spying on us, you and me. I see strange men loafing around town."

"Yes. I didn't tell Sam but I saw them."

"We shouldn't be riding out to the cave."

"I know. That's what I wouldn't tell Sam also."

"It's too much," Piney said. "It's not good for you, for your health."

"If I don't ride out Sam will come in," she said. There was weariness, desperation in her.

"I'll make sure tomorrow and if they're spying I'll get word to Sam," he said.

"Yes. I guess you're right."

She was listless and quiet for the rest of the ride and when they had left the horses with Camponetta she went straight home. She did not look well, Piney thought. The strain was beginning to tell upon her. He felt little better himself, tossing in the bed all night. . . .

He awakened at his regular time, started the fire in the bath house. He ran short of wood and blinked into the early morning light, not yet sunshine. Someone darted out of sight behind the shed. He pretended not to notice, picking up an armful of sticks, returning to the shop. He was sweating despite the cool morning air.

He stacked the wood, feeling as though someone was watching him. He went to the front and applied his eye to the edge of the windowshade. A stranger was sitting on the edge of the walk opposite, picking his teeth. At the corner of Wayne and Main streets there was another of them looking toward Alicia's house. Piney drew a deep breath and went to his stove to cook his breakfast. He would have to act in a totally normal manner, he knew, following the daily routine so that they would not be aware that he was onto them.

He took his bath and promptly at nine o'clock he raised the windowshade and unlocked the door. Lige Tinsley and John Stang stepped inside. Tinsley leaned against the door and through the window Piney could see Masters and California and the stranger from across the street. He did not need to be told that the back door was guarded in the same manner. He looked quickly toward his rifle—it was too far away.

Stang said in his heavy voice, "Night-ridin' last night, was you, Talcott?"

"That's right." There was no use in denial.

"Kay Cross lost some prime beef last night."

"Is that so? You don't think I stole it?"

"I think you was ridin' with a white lady," Tinsley said savagely. "Where I come from that'd get you tarred, feathered and hung."

"You'd better ask the lady about that." He was scared but he knew he had to stand up to them.

"I intend doin' just that," said Stang. "Lige, here, he's sweet on the lady. I ain't. What I want from you, nigger, is the whereabouts of Sam Booker. I want his hideout. I want a map so we can ride right up to it."

"That's something I wouldn't know about."

For a big man Stang moved with amazing speed. The hard palm of his right hand struck alongside Piney's head. It sent him reeling toward Tinsley.

"I don't want the black bastard." Tinsley laughed as he smashed Piney's nose, hurling him at Stang.

Stang held him at arm's length. "You want to talk or be kicked to death?"

Blood ran from Piney's nose, inside his lacerated cheek. Deep, inherited fear, relic of three hundred years of oppression of his race by white masters, gripped his middle. He could not have spoken had he so desired. He saw Camponetta through the window, saw Masters lay his gun on the blacksmith. Tom Mason and others came but were held at bay. There was no hope of rescue, he knew.

Stang hit him in the belly. He doubled over and Stang's knee caught him and shot him upright. Tinsley hit him at the back of the neck and he fell forward, still conscious. They wanted him conscious he realized, they wanted to make him talk. He tried to fight back and they laughed, pitching him back and forth like a baseball, never quite knocking him out, hurting him. "A nigger hates bein' kicked in the shins," Tinsley said. He dug the heel of his boot so that Piney gasped and tears blinded him.

"That oughta do it," said Stang. "Don't kill him 'til he spits out the truth."

They slammed him into the barber chair, slapped him with a towel so that blood spattered. Tinsley spied a razor on the shelf, brandished it.

"Hey, looka here. He'll talk now. Otherwise I'll cut off an ear. Then the other ear. Then his black damn nose."

"I don't think it'll come to that," said Stang. "I reckon he'll speak a few words."

They stepped back from the chair, grinning, certain of themselves. Piney pushed with his feet and came off head first. He butted his skull into Tinsley's middle, knocking the breath out of him. He used his last remaining vestige of strength to lunge for the rifle in the corner.

Stang stuck out a foot and tripped him. When he went down, Stang kicked him in the crotch. He doubled up and moaned, tears, blood, and sweat running from his orifices.

Tinsley's nostrils were pinched in tight and white, his face was like a mask. He pulled his revolver and said thickly, "You seen it, John. You seen the nigger butt me. Now he's mine." He looked at the razor, at the gun. "I'll cut it out of him and then I'll blast him to hell."

Stang said, "He won't talk, Lige. I'm tellin' you he won't. He's got sand, I'll say that for him."

"Let him die, then." Tinsley stepped to where Piney's head lay hard against the floor. "You hear me, nigger? Talk, then die. Or die without talkin', I wouldn't give a hoot which. You hear me?"

The door banged open. Both Stang and Tinsley whirled in amazement. A skirted fury flew past them. Alicia dropped to her knees beside Piney.

"You rotten, dirty, low-lived skunks, you smelly, rotten filthy low-lives," she said. "Get out of here. Get out, do you hear me?"

Tinsley said, "Now, Alicia. . . ."

"Out!" She cradled Piney's head in her arms. "White men? He's ten times as white as you or your whore mothers!"

"Alicia!"

"You think I can't talk your language, you hogs? I've seen your kind in a dozen trail towns and cow camps. I've seen my father run your tails so far they caught fire. Out of here! Take your hired guns and leave this town."

"Now just a minute, Miss Maylan," said Stang.

She scrabbled across Piney and reached the rifle before they guessed her intent. She levered a shell into the chamber with the speed and dexterity of one who knew firearms. She held it waist level.

"How would you like it in the gut?" she demanded. "You ever see a man die of a gut wound? I did. It takes hours."

Tinsley muttered, "She's gone crazy."

"Yeah," said Stang wonderingly. "I never did see a woman like of this."

"Better go," said Tinsley. "We can get him later. Any time."

"Try it," she said. "Try and get him. If he lives this town will see that you don't get him. Go and kill people who won't fight back. Get out, I say!"

They backed out. On the walk, Masters said bewilderedly, "Gosh, I didn't know what to do. She charged right past me. I couldn't gun her, could I?"

"Mount up," said Stang. He was looking at the townspeople gathered on Main Street. They were not armed except with their accusing stares. "Pull the men in and head for the ranch. If it's war they want, it's war they'll get. Put the men back to work on that dam. There'll be no more water in the Valley exceptin' Kay Cross water. There'll be no more business in this town. We buy in Silver City. You hear that, all of you?"

Tom Mason said, "Quesada lived without you. Quesada will be here when you're gone."

"Like hell it will. Quesada is now dead. I pronounce it dead and I may bury it. Burn it and bury it."

Mason said, "Dr. Brown, are you there? Will you see to Piney, please?" He turned his back. The others followed, ignoring the Kay Cross men as they rode out of town in a body of clanking spurs and pounding hooves, the dust billowing in their rear.

Dr. Brown was an old man with a short beard. He had been in the Valley since the War and he knew as much about contusions and broken bones as any man could know. He examined Piney and shook his head.

"He'll be laid up some time. He needs constant care."

"But he'll—he'll be all right?" Alicia still clutched the rifle.

"Broken nose. Broken ribs. Bad bruises, maybe internal injuries. If we had a hospital, like I always been saying . . ."

"Take him to my house."

"Your house? But you can't do that, Lishia."

She said, "Is this my day for ordering men around? Casper, get a shutter. And a blanket. Take him to my house, I'll nurse him."

Camponetta said, "She is right. Do like she say."

Dr. Brown said, "Well, we need hot water and all . . . It's right noble of you, Lishia. With nursin', he's got a real fine chance. There'll be fever, always is. I'll leave a list of things and instructions."

"You do that." She gripped the rifle, following the men as they carried Piney to her house, to the spare bed in a tiny room off the kitchen. When they were gone and she finally sat down she was surprised to find that she still held the rifle. It was symbolic of the life she was leading, the woman she was becoming. She had always been vigorous, hence the long rides in the hills alone and with Ricco, the hunting of small game and cougar, the curiosity about the land and all that lived on it. Now it was all concentrated on the war in the Valley, on the protest against injustice, the determination to avenge her father—and her love for Sam Booker.

Piney groaned and she set the rifle in a corner and took up a soft cloth and warmed-up witch hazel. They had stripped him to the waist and she marveled at the softness of the black skin as she gently applied the balm as the doctor had suggested. She knew what some people would say and think about having the Negro in her home and she cared nothing about it. She had grown fiercely uncaring about the opinions of others.

She thought of rushing to Piney's defense and how the gunslingers had been startled out of their wits at her ferocity. She had known they would not physically prevent her, that the code of the time and place protected her, but above and beyond that her wrath had daunted them. Lige Tinsley would never again take her for granted and John Stang would have second, third and fourth thoughts about her.

The danger, she thought, was to Sam and Ricco and the imported gunnies. Not for a moment did she discount the power of Kay Cross, her father had warned her of it before his murder. There would be more and more pressure exerted as Stang called in his farflung army of men. One slip and they would come down on the meager crowd in the hills and wipe them out.

She knew what she would do in that case. She looked at Piney's rifle, at her own light piece. If they killed Sam she would have no reason for living. Kay Cross would have to go down infamously as the outfit that killed a woman in self defense.

It was a week before Sam came into Quesada on another moonless night with the storm clouds swirling and a high wind blowing. With the lights out the three of them talked in the room where Piney lay recovering from his beating.

Piney said weakly, "I shouldn't be here. I want her to take me home."

"She's right," said Sam. "Doc wants you watched day and night."

Alicia said, "Sam, you look terrible. What happened?"

"Been on the run," he said. "They caught me in the open and cut me off from the cave. Had to ride a hundred miles in the hills without food, couldn't make a fire. Lost 'em, finally and detoured back."

"There are too many of them. They'll find the cave."

"They'll die if they do."

"All of them?"

"Enough of them." He looked at Piney and tears came to his eyes. "If I can get Stang and Tinsley I won't give a damn."

"They come in every day. They ride through town and the people see them and worry. Stang threatened to burn the town and it sticks in their craw."

"Has everyone got a gun?"

"The store sold out, guns and cartridges."

"Then there's hope," said Sam. "If the town quit, it would be all over. I've seen towns cowed by a mob. It's the most scarey thing in the world."

Piney whispered, "Have we got the right? I mean, is it right to put the town in danger?"

"It would be in worse trouble without us," Sam said.

"I guess you're right," Piney said. "I guess it would be downed without a struggle." He closed his eyes.

Alicia beckoned and Sam followed her into the other room, enfolded her in his arms, and kissed her long and hard. She responded, breaking for a moment, moaning her desire and bereavement and loneliness into his ear. Then she braced herself and leaned hard against him and managed a small laugh.

"They're out there all around us. If they could see us!"

"They can't and they won't. Benson got back. Across the border there are plenty of buyers, they hate Kay Cross. They smear the brand and drive them deeper into Mexico. Shag and his boys are right happy. We're goin' to hit 'em again, maybe tonight."

"But you need rest. I can see it."

"Who can rest? Can you sleep?"

"Not very well."

"There's too many pictures dancin' in a body's mind."

"Yes. Too many pictures." She kissed him again.

An hour later he slipped out the rear door. He remained motionless in the deep shadow for a moment. He had acquired the sixth sense of a hunted beast, he thought. He could detect no human noise among the night sounds, could see no one. He made his way across an empty lot to Camponetta's smithy where he had left his horse.

Now there was the odor of danger, he smelled it on the night. He drew his revolver and flattened himself against the wall of the smithy. Two men were coming from opposite directions, stealthily, carrying shotguns. He held his breath and waited. He could never beat a crossfire between two such weapons, he knew. He thought of Zeke Maylan and the way it must have been with him. He wished he had his rifle, so that he might try each adversary with two guns at the same time.

Then he realized they had not yet spotted him. They may have seen him but they could not locate him. He pushed his shoulder blades against the building and held the Colt waist-high, trying to watch both at once. One of them whistled, the other responded, a bird call.

He had them in the line of his peripheral vision now. If he could be dead sure that they were enemies and not citizens on patrol he could shoot first and take his chances. It was not in him to do this, he had not reached the stage of utter lawlessness and callousness. He waited agonizingly.

Suddenly one of the men went from view. It was as if a giant hand had snatched him down. The other said hoarsely, "Harding? What's up, Harding."

It was enough, Harding was a name well-known to Sam Booker. He stepped away from the wall and said, "Here I am, sucker."

The second man whirled but Sam shot him down and the gun clattered from his hands. Immediately Sam ducked and whirled, changing position.

Camponetta said, "I have got this one. Bring them inside, Sam."

Relief flooded him with sweat. He went to where the man he had shot lay on his back and took him by the boot heels and dragged him inside the blacksmith shop. Camponetta carried Harding in like a sack of potatoes and dropped him alongside his friend.

"I think his neck is broke," said the blacksmith. "I was waiting for you, they came."

"Saved my bacon, too. I owe you for it."

"My boy Ricco is with you. What else could I do?"

No one had been aroused by the single shot, evidently, or if awake had not cared to dare the dark streets where Kay

Cross men skulked. Sam examined Harding and found that his neck was indeed broken by the hands of the sturdy Camponetta.

"We better get rid of them," he said.

"We bury them. See? The manure heap?"

There was a huge pile of manure behind the shop, useful as fertilizer. They took shovels and made an excavation, then dug into the soft earth and made a hole large enough for the two bodies. It took an hour and both were sweating when it was done.

"Beneath the manure," said Camponetta. "A good place for such swine."

"We found two in the hills, these two can join 'em in hell."

"Ricco found them. He is well, Ricco?"

"He is fine. And without him we'd be no place. I tried to keep him out of it, you know. He wouldn't leave."

"It is his duty. I am proud of him. Oh, I worry and his mama weeps. But he does what he must."

"I won't be comin' in again," Sam said, knowing it was the truth and that he was right. "Tell Alicia. I can't bring danger to you people."

Camponetta was holding the two shotguns. He said, "She will be very sad. But you are correct." He held out the guns. "These I will add to my armor. Right?"

"Right," said Sam. "Be real careful, now."

"God be with you."

He rode out the roundabout way, avoiding the regular highway. Ricco had taught him all the shortcuts and indirect, concealed trails, some old Apache trails, some Ricco had himself broken in his hunting days. He would not see Alicia soon, he thought. He would not see Piney. He was both hunter and hunted and sooner or later Kay Cross would find him, as tonight, and there would be more killing. And sooner or later his luck had to change. He only prayed he would line up Tinsley and Stang before he died.

CHAPTER EIGHT

The springtime slowly turned to summer that year as Piney fought to regain health and strength. Everything that happened filtered through to him sooner or later . . .

Kay Cross sent its herd up the trail to Silver City guarded by fifty riders. A battle ensued and three more herders were killed. Sam Booker's men were reported to have suffered injuries, possibly death but the truth could not be learned since they appeared, reappeared, finally vanished carrying their wounded. It was sworn that they had been joined by Indians and Silver City people were worried about an uprising. . . .

Fresh Kay Cross cattle brought in for the grama grass were raided time and again. Two of Booker's cohorts were finally caught and hanged despite efforts to rescue them. The next night four Kay Cross gunslingers were ambushed and shot down and the one who escaped thought he recognized Sam Booker and the notorious Shag Benson among the avengers. . . .

Kay Cross cut off all business with the people of Quesada. The town's economics were seriously hurt—but when the dam was completed and the farmers began to suffer it would be disastrous. There were signs that the morale of the town was cracking around the edges. People like Finnegan the saloonkeeper and Otto Mueller the owner of the general store were fomenting the notion of capitulating to the enemy . . .

Tom Mason and Casper the carpenter and Camponetta the blacksmith stood firm against Kay Cross but it was difficult to distinguish how many of the other townsfolk and farmers would—or could—remain staunch . . .

Kay Cross brought in range detectives and more gunslingers. Some of them were suspected but not identified so that Valley people lived in constant discomfort lest they be always under surveillance. As summer approached the tensions mounted, grew enormous. . . .

Piney became able to rise from his bed of pain. His first

look into a mirror shocked him to his core. His nose was flattened and twisted to one side. One ear was bunched like that of a prizefighter. An eyebrow was scarred and his upper lip marred. His ribs still ached and there was a pain in the groin. He fell back into bed and wept, not because he had been rendered ugly but because his feeling of inadequacy had weakened his resistance. Only the attentions of Alicia pulled him through this period. . . .

Alicia grew thin and careworn. She did not see Sam for weeks, the news was sketchy and always late, she never knew the actual day's happening in the war. She lavished care upon Piney, giving him all the tenderness she felt for Sam . . .

The day came when Piney could hobble down Main Street. Alicia protested but Dr. Brown, knowing the townspeople, knowing his patient, encouraged him to creep into his shop and take rest in his own bed with Mason and others now taking over much of Alicia's former duty. He gradually became strong enough to stand, then to attend the shop part time, finally full time. There was not as much business as before, Quesada people were forced to save their pennies in the face of the slumping economy . . .

Lige Tinsley came no more to court Alicia but she began to ride the hills again at night. She was familiar with all the trails but everyone was against her daring except Piney, who knew her now, knew she had to try and reach Sam Booker, that her life was nothing unless she could make contact with her lover. She was successful to a degree as summer came on; it gave her release to ride even though she was cut off from the cave by watchers. She carried her rifle ready in the boot and a shotgun across her saddle. She was changing too, becoming quiet and haunted, her eyes huge in new hollows, her cheekbones prominent, her mouth too often a straight line. . . .

The night came when Piney was prone upon his bed with his own inner problems, the shop closed. He was utterly weary but stronger, he thought, than the past week. As always his hands, barber's hands, were steady while he quaked within. A familiar knock at his door brought him to his feet. He admitted Alicia, home from a ride, in dark men's attire. She accepted coffee and sank into his one comfortable chair, long slim legs extended, her face empty. His heart turned over the sight of her.

"I couldn't get past them," she said dully.
"There's so many of them."
"More and more. Sam is getting desperate. Benson has been unable to recruit more men. They're all scared. Kay Cross has put out the word they'll be hunted and hanged."
Piney unfolded a piece of paper in the form of a "Wanted" dodger. "This was posted on the Wells Fargo wall. Tom Mason brought it to me."
It was rudely lettered in black ink but the message was clear enough:

PROSCRIBED
Sam Booker
Ricco Camponetta
Shag Benson
and others riding with Booker, including Indians
AND
The Town Of Quesada
All of the above wanted for trial for murder, arson and rustling cattle in this Valley.
REWARDS
of $5,000 each for them named above and $500 each for any other persons proved to be one of Booker's bunch.
Signed:
Kay Cross Ranch

"Tom tore it down but it's probably in Silver City, Deming, El Paso, every place around," said Piney. "It'll bring bounty hunters. There's nothing lower than a bounty hunter."
Alicia said, "Sam killed one of them last week. He knew the man, caught him stalking the cave."
"If one man can find the cave—then another can, too."
"Sam has killed too many men," said Alicia. "His hate is eating him."
"Can you blame him?"
"You hate them. But it doesn't change your being, your soul."
"It changes everyone. It must change us, this awful hatred."
"Sam is different. He—he's like a wild animal. Maybe because we can't see an end to it. The courts at Santa Fe haven't moved to grant a new injunction, to enforce the old one. Sam feels that papa died for no reason."
Piney said, "Alicia, when I was a boy the Civil War ended and men came home to New York. In my father's shop I

saw them. Young men with the faces of old men. With an arm or a leg gone. It seemed half the veterans had lost an arm or a leg. They talked. There was no glory in the war for them, no reason. They hated. They hated what had happened to them."

"But they didn't hate the enemy," she said.

"You're right there," he admitted. "It was war they hated."

"Sam hates Kay Cross. He hates Stang and Tinsley and Masters and their people. He lies awake figuring how he can get to them and kill them."

"He can't see any other ending to it," Piney said. "And God help us all, neither can I."

She said, "Don't lose hope, Piney. You're the only one who has held hope. I can't go on without you."

"I have hope. It's just that I can't figure a way," he told her. "Kay Cross won't talk terms, that's over. There's been too much bloodshed. But we're right and they're wrong. Maybe God can find a way."

"I don't know much about God," said Alicia. "We never were church people. But if He's up there, I pray He'll find the way."

She went out into the night. He took the revolver and after a moment he followed. They had both adopted dark clothing for the night, for movement without detection, they were two shadows, one following the other. She went the back ways and he stalked her, alert for Kay Cross spies.

Shadows, he thought, and Piney Talcott the blackest of them. He was learning to move like the cats who prowled the alleys. He saw her go into the house and sighed with relief. There were sounds from Finnegan's saloon, the gunslingers had to take their fun where they found it, hired hands with no goal, nothing in the past nor the future, "like an old army mule," Sam had said.

He made his way back to the shop and bolted the door. He put down the revolver and prepared for sleep. And what was there ahead for him, he added to his thoughts? The town nigger, making his obeisance to one and all while his heart ached and his bile choked him and fear coiled like a snake in his belly, fear for Sam—and for Alicia.

Because heaven help him he loved Alicia Maylan, not as a sister or a friend or the affianced of his partner but as a man. Nothing more frightening nor awful could have happened to him, he thought.

The way she had nursed him, the touch of her hands upon his sore body, her devotion, utter and skilful, her courage and her beauty, how could he help loving her? She was everything that a woman could be.

Not that she would ever know. The very notion would scare her worse than it did him. It would scare Sam—and amaze him, too. Not even Sam could in his wildest dreams imagine that a black man could honorably love a white woman. Rape they understood, they believed every Negro desired the body of a white woman. They could never understand that to the black man their white skin was pallid, lifeless, that the occasional rape was born from a different source, from the oppression which sent a man into craziness, into violence for the sake of defiant violence. No, it was not Alicia's white body that he loved, it was her being, her special kind of thoughts and actions, her character.

Yet he could not in the night, alone in his bed, forget the body, the hands which had nurtured him. He would be a liar if he said this was true. He could only hug it to himself and sometimes drop a tear upon his pillow even as he castigated himself for a violation of his friendship with Sam and Alicia's utter trust in him, Piney Talcott.

Leaving the cave for the raid Sam Booker said, "It's gettin' tougher, Shag."

"Sure is. I'm havin' a bit o' trouble with the boys. Too many guns. If you hadn't nailed that bounty hunter we might all be dead by now."

"Ain't much I can say." He looked uneasily at the cloudy sky. They always picked moonless nights to attack. "Them clouds are blowin' over."

"The boys want action," said Benson. "If we could cut out a good bunch and fatten up the purse they'd feel like they're gettin' some place."

"No more'n natural," Sam admitted. "Cooped up here, it's no fun for 'em."

"They think about them Kay Cross gunnies down in town boozin' it up, you know how it is."

"Right. Let's hope we get lucky tonight." He dropped back along the line of horsemen. The Kid, Wooden and Cactus were still with them and a half dozen others, some of whose names Sam could not remember. His mind was fuzzy tonight, he felt the pressure as never before. Alicia had been sad and too quiet when she had visited him earlier.

Ricco rode beside him, saying, "It's not a good night for it, Sam."

"I know."

"The high wind is blowing around the mountain tops."

"I told Benson."

"We have hit this pasture too often."

"I know. But the road to the border is most handy from there. They make a quick run with guns in the rear guard and they think that's the best way."

"Sam?"

"Yes, Ricco?"

"We have lost control of this."

"You think so?"

"I do not like it at all, Sam. Sure, we need help. But the help is runnin' the shebang."

"I'm beginnin' to feel the same way." But how was he to get out of it? He had no qualms about rustling Kay Cross cattle nor of shooting Kay Cross men. An eye for an eye, a tooth for a tooth, especially when there was no recourse in the courts. It was the law of the west, the law he knew and Kay Cross knew and which both sides accepted. He had no diminishing of spirit, he was merely weary of it, of the wild life in the hills, of the constant warfare twenty-four hours per day seven days per week. He was tired of being separated from Alicia, from the companionship and wisdom of Piney. He felt lost and far from home.

He said, "Ricco . . . Don't forget your orders."

"Not like to," said the youth.

"You're the one to carry the news to Alicia and Piney."

"I can't forget."

"No use to get killed out here. Get to town and maybe Piney can do somethin' for Alicia."

"I will do it."

"They got Clancy down in that pasture, you know. If we could cut him out and drive him safe away I'd feel my luck was turnin'," said Sam. "I know that's plumb silly but Clancy has been my luck."

"They got all your cattle down there now. We were just lucky they didn't find the cave."

"They will. Sooner or later it's got to be a showdown. These boys will fight but only for their lives, we know that."

"Only you and me have the real reason," Ricco agreed.

It had been inevitable that Kay Cross should find the little herd and Clancy in the dead end canyon. There was no way to hide cattle from so many riders. Yet it had hit Sam hard to find them gone, driven to the south pasture. It was one of the reasons he had reluctantly consented to this night's raid—the other being that he felt he could not refuse Benson and the restless wild riders their excursion across the border.

Now, as Ricco had said, it seemed wrong. The sounds of the creaking leather of saddle, the jingle of spurs, the breathing of horse and man on the high night air was no longer exhilarating, the spirit of adventure was missing. Sam tried to whisper himself out of despondency and failed. They came down a different way, over the grass, avoiding the trail in a parabola Ricco had laid out to escape possible ambush and there was the herd, dim shapes, new cattle from the far-flung Kay Cross empire. And there was Clancy, disdainful of the steers and another bull, ruling over the cows.

Benson said, "All right, hit 'em."

They rode down, shooting, looking for the customary two or three herders. They spread out fanwise and hoorawed at the cattle, intending to start them southward.

A blaze of fire came from what seemed to be all points of the compass. Benson yelled high and shrill like the Rebel he had been. And then the wind swept away the clouds from the moon and Sam could see it all.

There were Kay Cross men prone and shooting on the north side of the herd from whence they had figured the attack would come. There were twenty or thirty of them, maybe more.

Sam shouted, "Ricco, get goin'."

Ricco did not hesitate, he knew his job. He was gone on the swift black, bent over the pommel, flying to the trails he knew, heading back toward Quesada.

Sam emptied his rifle. There was not time to reload. He drew the revolver. He saw Shag Benson go down, his mount rolling over on him. He saw the Kid and Wooden drive straight into the guns to certain death.

His mind raced, thinking that this was the end of it, of the hopeless, footless dream of his own ranch, his own place, of marriage and a family and old Clancy out in the field making new calves every season; this was the finish and a bad one in this south pasture trying to steal cattle. He peered into the moonlight, which distorted the range, gave an unnatural appearance to the scene.

He heard Stang roar in his giant's voice, "Git Booker. Whereat's that bastard Booker?"

He shouted in a voice he did not recognize, "I'm comin' at you, you dirty bastard yourself sonofabitch."

He spurred toward the voice and there was Tinsley and Masters, too and the others of that bunch protecting the owners of Kay Cross. He fired and saw one of them go down, he thought it was Cooky Harris. Then his horse was hit and stumbled and a bullet took Sam in the thigh while he was in mid-air and when he landed on head and shoulder he felt the earth fall away until there was a huge hole and he went hurtling down into his hole full of thick black and then mercifully he neither knew nor cared for a time . . .

When he awakened he heard the heavy voices in debate. His head spun around and his leg had begun to ache. He tried to move but they had tied his hands behind him and fastened his ankles together.

Masters said, "God damn it he killed Cooky. There's plenty of trees betwixt here and town. Hang the bastard."

Tinsley said, "Best to get it over with, John. We got him cold tryin' to rustle cattle, that's a hangin' offense."

"No," said John Stang.

"But why the hell not?"

"Because he's the only one we got. The others are dead or run away."

"What the hell we want with him?"

"We want law and order in the Valley. We want the court in Santa Fe to have a leg to stand on. Them judges won't stay bought unless you give 'em something."

"What you givin' 'em? Might's well be a corpse."

"I got word a Jedge Carter is comin' to Quesada. He had some dealin's with Zeke Maylan. I don't know the man but we bring him a rustler all neat and with witnesses and all, plus the dead body of Shag Benson and what's he goin' to do? He's goin' to hang Sam Booker. All nice and legal."

"He a real judge?"

"He's comin' to hold court, that's real enough for me."

"I say hang the bastard," Masters said. "He killed too many of our people."

"You shut your mouth. Put him in the wagon with the

deaders and if anything happens to him on the way in, you better make tracks, Jake," Stang said. "This here is just what we need, a legal position in the Valley. Now you do like I say."

They picked Sam up and shoved him into the wagon body. The smell of new death and blood was all around him. The moon lit the face of Shag Benson, eyes staring, mouth open. The jolting ride to town began and for the first time in his life Sam Houston Booker fainted dead away.

Ricco crouched in Piney's barber shop. "I don't know about Sam. I saw Benson get hit. I did like Sam said, I lit a shuck for you all. Now I'll go scoutin' and see if I can find him."

Alicia was as white as the towel Piney gave her to bathe her face and stem her tears. "Is there a chance?"

"We rode right into 'em, Lishia," Ricco said. "They must've been waitin' there for days—nights, that is, 'cause I didn't see them daytime when I was looking for Clancy and our herd."

Tom Mason and Camponetta came into the shop. There were Kay Cross men on Main Street but none interfered. Casper came in and reported that a rider had spurred a lathered horse into town and that there was a celebration going on in Finnegan's saloon. They told him the news and he bowed his head and leaned hard against the wall.

"They got us," said Mason. "They got the Valley."

"Judge Carter sent me a telegram," Alicia said. "If I'd only got it earlier."

"It's just no use," Casper said dully. "Without Sam we got no way to fight them. The dam—they got the water, everything. The farmers are ready to move out."

"That's right," said Mason. "They won the war, it's over."

Ricco said, "They didn't win me. I can live in those hills forever."

"Is that a life?" asked his father. "Forever is a long, long time, my son. They can keep you there forever."

Mason said, "No use to sacrifice any more."

Now Otto Mueller crowded in and the banker and two or three others. The barber shop acquired the atmosphere of a funeral parlor. They should be meeting at Casper's place, Piney thought. He had eyes only for Alicia, seeing her at last brought down, defeated. It was because she believed Sam was dead, he thought. She could not, would not go on without Sam. His heart was wrenched at the sight of her, shoulders bowed, unable to stop weeping. He walked out of the shop into the street. Although the hour grew late people were gathering, talking in undertones among themselves. He walked among them and heard them and it was the sound of weeping, as Alicia was weeping. He went back to the shop.

They were now silent. Piney put his back against the front door and looked at them.

"We have talked before," he said. "We had hopes."

The scars on his face, his twisted nose reminded them of what had happened to him in his defiance, he felt. He wiped a hand over his chin.

He said, "If Kay Cross takes over you will all live as slaves. It's a funny thing. I'm a black man and I never did live as a slave."

Their eyes *slewed* away. Mueller cleared his throat but did not speak. Mason moved restlessly, Ricco laughed a short, bitter guffaw.

Piney said, "My people were slaves. They were brought to America as slaves. It is not a good way of life. You can ask any nigger in Texas or the Deep South. It's not a good way of life for blacks nor whites."

"Now, it won't be that bad," said Mason. "You can do business with John Stang."

"You could do business with Benedict Arnold," Piney told him. "To me, there is no way to do business with Kay Cross. This town has been good to me, a black man. I hoped to live my days out here. So if there are only going to be a few more days, then so be it."

"What do you mean, Piney? What can you do?"

"Kay Cross will ride in. Big and bold now that Sam is gone. Oh, they'll want to do business. Buy things from Mueller, establish themselves in Quesada again. They won't burn the town now because they can own it. You don't burn what you own. One way or another they will make it all seem legal. Then they will rule. And you'll be slaves."

"But you can't fight them."

"No. Not alone. But I can die trying to fight them. They killed Marshal Maylan. They killed Jack Delaney. And now they've killed Sam Booker. Oh yes, I can fight them until they kill me, too."

Against the rear wall Alicia stiffened. She stared at Piney. "He means it. He'll do it." Her voice rose.

Ricco said, "Everybody owns guns. What happened to you? We talked about it. What happened?"

"We had Sam," said Mason. "Sam was the leader."

"I'm no leader," said Piney. "But I'm willing to die rather than be a slave."

Their faces altered in small ways. Even Otto Mueller began to assume the expression of a determined boar. Mason lighted up and was about to speak.

That was when Kay Cross rode into town with the wagon containing the bodies and the one wounded survivor of Sam Booker's bunch, Sam himself. The people in the streets fell back and stared as Stang and Tinsley sat their horses and the riders gathered around them like a small army and Masters picked up Sam and slapped him to consciousness and propped him between himself and Jose California for all to see him bloodcaked and scarcely able to understand what was taking place.

Someone blew out the lamps in the barber shop. Alicia and Piney stood, hands entwined, rigid with surprise and relief.

Piney said, "Ricco, hide yourself . . . I'll go with you." He ran to his rifle. He shoved a razor into the pocket of his loose jacket. He handed his revolver to Tom Mason.

"You may have to use it, I know you don't own one," he said, his voice sharp and clear. "You can take your choice, use it on Kay Cross, throw it away—or use it on Tommy and yourself. Because there'll be hell to pay before they do what I think they plan to do about Sam."

Ricco was already out the back door. Piney took one more look around.

"You people here—you're the leaders. You might not realize it but you are. Go listen to Kay Cross and then make up your minds. Mine's already made up."

He ran outside and said to Ricco, "The roof. There's a way up, see?"

There was a sturdy rainpipe and the stanchions made a sort of ladder which could be mounted by anyone of agility. On the roof, which slanted to the rear of the shop for drainage, was the usual false front parapet. It made a useful place of concealment for the two of them. They could look down and see plainly what was taking place on Main Street.

It had become an eerie scene. Kay Cross had brought

torches of tar and pine. Riders in a semi-circle blocked the west end of town, bearing the flickering brands to throw a ghost dance of shadows on people and buildings. Stang had mounted to the wagonbed where Sam still hung suspended between Masters and California. The entire town was banked along the walks and in the dust. Those who had been in the barber shop formed a tight group just beneath Piney and Ricco.

Piney said, "If they saw you they'd shoot. If they got me, they'd throw me in with my partner."

"We can take to the hills together," said Ricco. "We can get clear out of the country."

"Do you want to go?"

"Hell no. I want to shoot those bastards from here. I want to kill them all."

"We'd be cut down before we got them all."

"Yeah. But wouldn't it be great?" He sighted on the wagon with the rifle. "I could get Stang and Tinsley. You could get Masters and California."

"And Sam would be dead inside ten seconds."

"Yeah. But it would be great."

"Better to wait. There's Alicia."

"Yeah. There is Alicia."

"Better to lay low and wait."

"Yeah. But it would be great." Ricco lowered the rifle and Stang's voice rose above the murmur of crowd noise.

"This here town was pronounced dead. This here town gave shelter to cattle thieves and killers. Now I want you to see what happens to rustlers and murderers."

Two Kay Cross men handed the body of Shag Benson to another pair on the street. The torches shone on the dead face. A gasp, then a sigh rose from the populace of Quesada. One by one the Kid, Wooden, Cactus and a strange rider were lined up beside Benson.

Ricco said, "They left their own gunnies behind. They're not showing the ones we killed. Somebody might recognize them for what they were—outlaws."

"Where's Alicia? I don't see her."

"Seems like she'd be fightin' to get to Sam."

"It wouldn't do any good. See the way they've got everyone blocked off? She wouldn't get away with it this time. There's too many guns staring down the throats of the town."

Stang was waving his arms. "There's one missin' and you

all know who he is. The blacksmith's own boy. Ricco Camponetta. He's as guilty as the rest of 'em. And now here is the leader, the one that broke the peace of this here Valley—there he is, folks, look at 'im. Sam Booker."

The murmur rose. Sam's face was ashen, his eyes barely slitted, his shoulders drooping.

"We got him alive. We goin' to keep him alive. We goin' to have law in this here Valley," Stang roared. "Real law. The law of the range. We didn't hang this here rustler, no sir. We brought him in and we goin' to try him. There's a jedge comin' to Quesada. We goin' to hang Sam Booker."

Someone shouted "No!" and guns swung in the direction of the voice and again there was silence.

Stang said, "Oh, yes we are. We goin' to hang him legal. We caught him dead to rights, we got fifty witnesses. We goin' to hang him by the neck 'til he's dead, dead, dead."

A woman wept, it was not Alicia, Piney knew. It was a a huge temptation to give Ricco the word, to draw a bead on Stang and Tinsley and the others and shoot them down. But he knew the result would be a holocaust, with innocent people dying in the dust on Main Street.

"That's law," Stang was orating. "Now Kay Cross has got somethin' to say to you people. You take the boy, Ricco. He was drug into crime by Sam Booker. Let him come in and confess and let him bear witness against Sam Booker and repent—and Kay Cross will defend him and when he serves his little time, Kay Cross'll give him a job. That's the kind of people Kay Cross is."

Camponetta said firmly, "Ricco will not betray his friend."

Stang said, "Then the law will get Ricco some day. Further and more, there's a nigger somewhere in this town. He's a pardner to these crimes. We want him. We aim to try him along with Sam Booker. We aim to hang him as high as his pardner."

Ricco said, "Hey, Piney, how 'bout that? Me, I only go to jail. You get to hang with Sam. They're discriminatin' against me."

Piney said, "He's trying hard to play it smart. He'd have a case in court with all his false witnesses."

As if to prove Piney correct Stang's voice altered, the stern lines of his face softened. "Now I wanta tell you citizens of Quesada, you Valley people here, the sentence on this town is lifted. Anything was said before, just forget it. The jedge is comin', everything is goin' to be all shipshape. We only want what's right. When these here rustlers is hung Kay Cross will begin doin' business here again and all is goin' to be fine and dandy in this here country."

"Damn decent of you, Stang," cried a voice and again the muzzles of the guns swung around.

People began drifting, now. They did not go home, they simply drew apart, eyes on the unconscious Sam Booker. Lige Tinsley came forward toward the barber shop, paused in front of Tom Mason.

"Mason, I understand you got the keys to the jail."

"The jail is town property."

"And we got a town jailbird." Tinsley held out his hand. "You better hand 'em over. Otherwise we got to take 'em."

Mason took out the keys, hesitated, then shrugged and gave them to Tinsley.

Stang was saying, "You all got a doctor in this here town. Better send him to the jailhouse. We want Booker alive for the hangin', now, don't we? All legal like. Sure we do, and then everything's goin' to be fine."

Piney said, "We'd better make ourselves scarce before they start looking for us."

Ricco said, "Don't worry about me. I got more places to hide than they can dream of. I'll be around, Piney. No matter what happens, I'll be around."

He went down from the roof and vanished. Piney followed. They were already hammering on the door of the barber shop. He went the familiar back way, circled and came to Alicia's small house. He crept to a window and was about to open it. From above him Alicia's voice was a cool whisper.

"I've been waiting for you."

He climbed into the darkened house. "They'll be here—Tinsley will be here."

"Yes." She clutched his hand. "But we have time to talk, make plans."

"Not much time. But I have a plan—I think."

"The town—we can't count on the town."

"Can you blame them? All those guns. And Stang claiming a judge is coming to hold court."

"The judge is coming, you know."

"To what? Lies backed by witnesses. No, we've got to do something quick."

"Tonight?"

"If Sam wasn't wounded. We'll have to wait 'til Dr. Brown has attended him."

"Early morning?"

"We'll have to break into the jail somehow. Ricco will be nearby. We can get away."

She moved to a drawer in the kitchen. "We won't have to break in. I have a set of keys I forgot to leave."

"Wonderful! Maybe that's a good luck sign."

Her voice shook. "Did you see Sam? How pitiful he looked? His leg—his poor leg. Will he be able to ride?"

"That's what we've got to chance."

"Where can we hide?"

He said, "I used to read a lot. Most everything. A man named Poe, Edgar Allen, wrote a story. It was about a letter. Nobody could find it because it was right under their noses."

"Yes?"

"They already searched my shop."

She said, "I'm ready. I dressed for it. I have papa's guns. I only wish I could see Sam."

"If you visit Sam they've got you."

"I know." She sighed as though her heart was bursting. "Should we go now?"

"I think we'd better. Tinsley will be looking for you."

They went out the back door and over the dark, hidden byways to the barber shop. Piney reconnoitered to see if a guard had been left within. The sound of celebration had resumed at Finnegan's saloon and the shop was empty. Kay Cross, he thought, was contemptuously confident. If only the town would rally against them . . .

The town was without blame, he repeated. There were women and children to be considered, there was property, everything they owned, there was a common respect for law, possibly hope that the judge would somehow bring justice to the Valley. He removed the sheets from his cot and replaced them with fresh ones. His clock told him that it was after one in the morning.

He said, "Will you try to sleep, Alicia?"

"I can't sleep."

"You've got to try. I'll watch. I can't leave this room, they could see me. I don't dare lower the shade or close the door—they'd know I'd been here."

She said, "I'll lie down. Do you think we can get him out, Piney?"

"We'll manage somehow." He thought that he would probably manage to get himself killed and that there was great danger to her also, she was wearing the dark men's clothing. He knew there was no way to prevent her from trying to free Sam and no use to discuss it.

She stretched herself on the bed with a small groan. He could dimly see her profile, clean and lovely. He busied himself with weapons, her father's sawed-off shotgun, the rifle, the revolvers, placing them all at hand. If they came through the door he would have to shoot even while Alicia escaped through the rear. He placed the jail keys at bedside where she could grab them if necessary. He hoped he had thought of everything possible.

He tried to think even harder, so that he would not think about the woman on his bed.

He wondered where Ricco was at this moment. The strategy for the early morning did not require the youth's presence but it would be much better if he were around at that time and if he could have recruited at least a few men of the town, like his father and Tom Mason and possibly Casper. He rested the rifle beside him and cradled the murderous shotgun across his knees and forced himself to stay awake and to ponder on the possibilities of the morning and to not look at Alicia.

CHAPTER NINE

At the first warning of dawn beyond the mountains when pale violet sprayed the town, Alicia and Piney ventured forth, again on the back ways of the town. Kay Cross had celebrated late with hard liquor and Quesada people had reason to remain indoors so that they felt easy about making it to the house behind the jail where the Maylans had resided.

There were clouds still in the sky. They scampered to the porch laden with their weapons and a key admitted them to the sitting room where they had spent so many hours together with Zeke and Sam planning the future of Razor

Edge. It was forlorn, empty of furniture, dust on the window-sills.

There was no time for sighs or fond memories. Piney led the way through the kitchen to the door that led to the jail cells. Alicia produced the key.

The door opened without a squeak of hinge as they knew it would—Zeke had always insisted upon having it oiled. They edged through. The guard was on the outside of a heavy hinged oaken door. Sam was lying in the cell nearest their end of the corridor.

He was wide awake. He looked at them without surprise. He grinned the old Booker grin, made a motion for silence, picked up his injured leg and dropped it over the side of the bunk. He grabbed a heavy walking stick which was recognizable as the one Dr. Brown always provided his gimpy patients.

Alicia worked with the big heavy key to the cell. Piney waited inside the big door, the barrel of the shotgun poised to strike if the guard heard the sound and became suspicious. The cell door swung open and Sam hobbled out and into Alicia's eager arms.

Piney tiptoed to them and motioned, giving Sam an arm. They made it back into the house and Alicia locked the door behind them. Even then they whispered.

"I knew you'd get here," said Sam, leaning on the cane, holding Alicia close with his other arm. "You got a gun for me, I hope."

"Papa's belt," she said, reluctantly squirming loose and adjusting it around his hips where it fit loosely but well enough. "Can you ride, darling?"

"Get me a horse and I'll ride. The bullet nicked the bone, Doc says, but I can ride."

Piney stood apart, watching them, the love that overflowed between them. He said dryly, "First we've got to get to Camponetta's. We didn't dare bring horses around here."

"Ricco?"

"He's outside somewhere."

"Thank God. I was afraid he was dead. I didn't see him last night."

"You mean you could see us," demanded Alicia. "But you seemed half dead yourself."

"I figured to fake it a little. I figured maybe they wouldn't watch so close if I was in bad shape. Doc Brown helped, told them I'd be in bed a week."

"Good. But we've got to cross the street somewhere to get to the smithy," said Piney. "Tell you what. We'll work our way opposite Camponetta's. Then I'll streak over. If I can pick up Ricco we can ride around town and come back to this side of Main Street and pick you up."

"I think we ought to stick together," said Sam dubiously. "More fire power with all these guns we got."

"No, Piney's right," said Alicia. "You can't move fast enough. And Ricco will be watching, you know how he is."

"Yeah. Ricco will be some place watching," agreed Sam. "Okay. Should we start before the sun gets over the mountains?"

He kissed Alicia and again they clung together. Piney swallowed hard and opened the door, looking up and down. There was no one in his view.

He said, "It's clear."

The purple of morning was laced with gold. It was a danger but it also allowed them to see the earth upon which Sam was forced to walk, to avoid trash in the back yards and empty lots, to step over or around the holes and mounds and tree stumps. Their progress was slow; Sam's brave words exceeded his strength, the leg hurt him and it showed on his face. He had aged, Piney thought, the lines from his nose to the corners of his wide mouth were trenches. Alicia supported him tenderly and at length they came opposite the blacksmith shop.

"If we only knew where Ricco is," said Alicia.

"He'll be there when he's needed," said Piney. "Now look, if they stop me don't start shooting. In case of Ricco, you see? In case he's got something."

"If they stop you. . . ." Sam broke off.

"On account of Alicia," said Piney. "You understand?"

"Not for me," she said.

"For you and the whole town. You saw those torches. If Quesada hadn't kept quiet they'd have burned us out."

"He's right," said Sam. "Piney's generally right." He stuck out a hand. "Bless you, pardner."

Piney said, "I'm going to sprint. I'm going fast, there's no cover for us. Just pray a little."

He gathered himself. He looked at the rifle in his hands,

shook his head. It would hamper his speed. He turned and handed it to Alicia. The way seemed clear.

He tugged at his belt and ran. His boots sent dust flying from the middle of Main Street. There was still no sign of Kay Cross men. He hit the boardwalk and the blacksmith shop yawned ahead of him, beckoning. The horses were stalled in the rear, he could hear the rattle of halters as they nibbled at the morning's hay.

He ran over the threshold of the shop, circled the anvil. He was reaching for the first saddle when Lige Tinsley's voice said, "Whoa, there, nigger."

He stopped dead. Turning slowly he saw Tinsley just inside the entry, lounging, grinning.

"Go for your gun, nigger, why don't you?"

"I don't have a gun," said Piney. His blood was congealing, he could feel the beginning of fear, his insides quaked once more.

"No, huh? Just like a damn black nigger. Knew you'd be lookin' for horses around here. Thought Kay Cross was all asleep, did you?"

Piney shrugged. It was over now so far as he was concerned. If only Ricco was watching and could get to Alicia and Sam, something might be saved.

He said, "What difference, you white bastard?"

Tinsley stalked forward and hit him a swinging blow. It knocked him out of the shop and into the street. He rolled over the boardwalk, knowing that he was seen by Alicia and Sam, knowing they would be aware of the situation. He got to his knees as Tinsley fired a shot, then another into the air and roared his command.

"All right Kay Cross. Up and at 'em. I got the damn nigger."

On his knees, wagging his head to clear the shadows, Piney saw Masters and California flanking Tinsley, grinning. Masters came toward him, rifle in hand.

Then he saw Sam. He moaned, "No, oh, no!"

Sam had broken away from Alicia. He had hobbled to the mouth of the alley, Zeke's gun dangling at his side. Supporting himself on the cane, his face white with thunderous rage, his right hand poised over the butt of the revolver.

Masters saw Sam at the same time, lifted the rifle. Piney's hand dipped into his pocket. He came up from his knees in one long, leaping move. The razor flashed in his expert, strong and nimble hand. He slashed once.

Masters screamed, dropping the rifle, yelled, "Lige!"

Tinsley, confused at Masters' howl, at the sight of blood gushing from his foreman's arm, came on the run.

Sam called to him, "All right, Tinsley. You and me for the jackpot."

Piney had not stopped moving. Jose California could not get the gun around before he was struck by the keen, wet blade. His right arm fell, his hand almost cut off at the wrist. His keening yell matched that of Masters as men piled out of the hotel, Finnegan's bar, Kay Cross men rubbing their eyes but armed for a fight.

Piney was sobbing in fear for Sam. He tried to get across the street in time, he did not know why or what he would do. He saw Tinsley go for his revolver.

Then he saw Sam's right hand move, saw it claw down, saw the old polished gun of the Marshal leap and speak with a loud report. He wheeled around.

Tinsley seemed to be through with his revolver, he seemed to be throwing it away. Both hands went to his belt. He doubled over and sank backwards, then rolled onto his side. Blood ran into the dust.

Scrambling, falling, rising, racing, Piney got to the alley-way. Alicia had come up with the guns, she thrust his rifle into his hands. Sam calmly holstered the pistol and accepted the big-mouthed riot gun.

"Couldn't stand still for him bad-mouthin' you like that, pardner," he said. "Wasn't goin' no place without you any old how."

Stang was in midstreet, waving his revolver, shouting, "Get 'em. They kilt Lige. Get 'em."

Kay Cross was coming, two score strong. There was no way to go, nowhere to run, Piney knew. Stang was the sole leader now, he was in charge, the others were down. The worst of them, Piney thought gratefully, Tinsley and his forever crippled badmen whose wrist tendons he had severed. For once he was thoroughly glad of his violence perpetrated on another human being, for once he was happy at the sight of blood and the dead body of Tinsley.

He said, "Alicia, please go. Ricco will be waiting."

"If they want to kill a woman," she said coolly, "let them be the first in the Southwest to do so."

She walked past them into the street with the rifle in her grasp and faced Kay Cross. They hesitated.

Stang roared. "Come on, she won't shoot nobody."

She pressed the trigger. A bullet kicked up dust at Stang's feet.

She said, "The next one's for my father. You want to take it, John Stang?"

His face went blood red in rage. He started to lift his sixgun.

From the roof of the hotel Ricco called, "Ho, Stang! Kay Cross! Look around you, big bad men?"

Stang whirled and stared. Ricco had a rifle pointed at him. From across the street, from every rooftop came hoots and yells. Stang wheeled around. Everywhere he looked there was a gun aimed at the Kay Cross men.

Tom Mason came into the street from his office. Casper flanked him and Otto Mueller. They were carrying arms. Little Tommy Mason staggered in their wake, a .32 pistol tightly clasped in both hands. Women came from the houses on the side streets carrying guns.

Stang's jaw hung down. Kay Cross men instinctively spread apart, ready for war.

Camponetta and his stout wife came from the blacksmith shop with guns. The banker walked out of the bank carrying a double-barreled shotgun. They all walked to where Sam and Alicia and Piney faced the Kay Cross people.

Dr. Brown walked among them. He knelt beside Tinsley, shrugged and went to where Masters moaned. He applied a tourniquet. He did the same for Jose California. Stang watched, fuming, his mind working so plainly that all could see it going around and around.

Sam said, "Looks like a Mexican standoff, John. You want a lot of blood or are you satisfied with what you got?"

Stang said, "You damn cow thief."

"The judge is comin'," Sam said. "You want to wait for him and a fair trial with Quesada people on the jury? Or do you want to die for Kay Cross?"

"You'll hang, I tell you."

"We're ready. How about you? I got you first," Sam told him.

Stang seemed to grow older on the moment. "You can't beat Kay Cross. We still own this here Valley."

"You think you do," said Sam. "Valley don't believe it.

You see these folks? See what kind of people they are? How you goin' to own these people, John?"

The big man wiped sweat from his red face. He said heavily, "All right, you men. Saddle up."

"That's a right smart order," Sam said. "Saddle up. Get back to your nest. When the judge gets here there'll be some changes made."

"You can't run Kay Cross into no corner."

"Kay Cross managed that its own self," Sam said. "Now I'll tell you what's goin' to happen. The judge is goin' to grant an injunction against your dam. Your boys there with the bum wings, they're goin' to be charged with the murder of Zeke Maylan and Jack Delaney. Could be you'll be called somethin'—what is it, Piney?"

"Accessory after the fact," said Piney.

"What he said. Piney, he reads a lot, he knows such matters."

"You turned thief and stole our cattle!"

"And in your south pasture is my bull Clancy and some Razor Edge stock."

"We was just carin' for 'em whilst you was in the hills raisin' hell."

"That was mighty nice of you," Sam said. "But we'll let the judge decide on that, too. Now if you want some good advice, John, you'll leave a short crew here. You and the rest of the boys will head out for El Paso. You can come back when the judge arrives. Meantime you ain't exactly safe hereabouts. I'm lookin' out for your health, John."

Stang had built an empire by using his brains, Piney thought. He was talking against the wind now, he had admitted defeat when he ordered Kay Cross men to saddle up.

"I'll do what I please when I please, Booker," Stang bluffed. But he turned his back and walked toward the hotel.

Sam faced the people of Quesada. His face worked for a moment, then his voice was controlled. "I thank you. I thank you with all my heart."

Tom Mason said, "Thank Piney. He showed us the way. When Ricco came with the plan we remembered what Piney said about being slaves."

Sam tried to take a step toward them and his leg buckled. Piney and Tom Mason caught him and carried him across the street and into the barber shop. They placed him in the barber chair. He grinned at them as Alicia came beside him and hugged him.

Piney said, "Sam, you sure need a bath a shave and a haircut. I'll give you a special rate today."

They could laugh heartily from the relief within them. Piney went into the bath house and gathered kindling. It would be all right now. The judge could marry them. He started the fire with the aid of a little coal oil to make it burn bright. The flame flickered and he reached into his pocket for a handkerchief to wipe the tears which were somehow on his cheeks.

They were tears of joy, of course. He was going to be able to spend his days on Razor Edge after all. He would live in his own little house and Alicia would raise children in the big house and he would ride the range with Sam and Ricco. It would be a fine life. He had earned it and in a white man's world.

When he put the kerchief away his hand encountered the old razor. He took it out and wiped it carefully. He would have to hone it now. It wasn't a blade he used on customers, it was his own private razor.

He went out to the others, smiling.

William R. Cox was born in Peapack, New Jersey. His early career was in newspaper journalism. In the late 1930s he began writing sports, crime, and adventure stories for the magazine market, and he made his debut as a Western writer with "Night of the Blood Bucket Raid" in *Dime Western* in the January, 1941 issue. It is worth noting that his Western story debut was with the first of several stories to feature a series character, Terry Glenn. During the 1940s Cox created a number of other series characters for the magazine market, most notably the Whistler Kid who appeared regularly in *10 Story Western* and Duke Bagley whose adventures usually were featured in *Star Western*. "The short story form was blissful until there were no markets," he once recalled. In the 1950s and 1960s Cox turned to television and wrote at least a hundred teleplays for such series as "Broken Arrow," "Dick Powell's Zane Grey Theater," "The Virginian," and "Bonanza." He also won a host of readers writing original paperback Western novels, the best known of which are novels about the adventures of two series characters originally published by Fawcett Gold Medal: Cemetery Jones in a series published under his own byline and the Tom Buchanan series which appeared under the house name, Jonas Ward. Dale L. Walker in the second edition of *Twentieth Century Western Writers* (1991) commented that William R. Cox's Western "novels are noted for their 'page-turner' pace, realistic dialogue, and frequent Colt-and-Winchester gun play. The series of novels built around the strong West Texas character, Tom Buchanan, are very typical Cox Western." Among his non-series Western novels, his most notable titles are *Comanche Moon* (1959), *The Gunsharp* (1965), and *Moon at Cobre* (1969).